SCENE OF THE CRIME: MEANS AND MOTIVE

New York Times Bestselling Author

CARLA CASSIDY

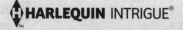

HARLEQUIN INTRIGUE®

To Bob and Jenny Offutt, thanks for the wonderful hospitality we received when we stayed with you at your beautiful resort, Crystal Cove Bed and Breakfast in Branson.

Recycling programs for this product may not exist in your area.

ISBN-13: 978-0-373-74994-2

Scene of the Crime: Means and Motive

Copyright © 2016 by Carla Bracale

HARLEQUIN®
www.Harlequin.com

Printed in U.S.A.

Carla Cassidy is an award-winning, *New York Times* bestselling author who has written more than one hundred and twenty novels for Harlequin. In 1995, she won Best Silhouette Romance from *RT Book Reviews* for *Anything for Danny*. In 1998, she also won a Career Achievement Award for Best Innovative Series from *RT Book Reviews*. Carla believes the only thing better than curling up with a good book to read is sitting down at the computer with a good story to write.

Books by Carla Cassidy

Harlequin Intrigue

Scene of the Crime

Scene of the Crime: Bridgewater, Texas
Scene of the Crime: Bachelor Moon
Scene of the Crime: Widow Creek
Scene of the Crime: Mystic Lake
Scene of the Crime: Black Creek
Scene of the Crime: Deadman's Bluff
Scene of the Crime: Return to Bachelor Moon
Scene of the Crime: Return to Mystic Lake
Scene of the Crime: Baton Rouge
Scene of the Crime: Killer Cove
Scene of the Crime: Who Killed Shelly Sinclair?
Scene of the Crime: Means and Motive

Visit the Author Profile page at
Harlequin.com for more titles.

CAST OF CHARACTERS

Jordon James—An FBI agent who has come to Branson to solve a trio of murders. She quickly becomes marked by the killer as the next victim.

Gabriel Walters—Chief of police. Can he protect Jordon from the killer and still hang on to his heart?

Kevin Rollings—The former owner of Diamond Cove. Has his need for revenge turned him into a cold-blooded murderer?

Ed Rollings—Is the handyman really doing his brother's dirty work?

Ted Overton—Has the present owner of the bed-and-breakfast hatched an evil plot to get his family back where they belong?

Billy Bonds—The groundskeeper has secrets... Is one of them deadly?

Chapter One

FBI Special Agent Jordon James hated two things—winter and murder—and she was about to be immersed in the middle of both. She frowned and stared out the small window of the helicopter that had carried her from Kansas City to the rousing tourist town of Branson, Missouri.

When they'd left Kansas City the ground had been winter brown and the temperature had been a balmy forty-five. Unfortunately, as they approached the Branson airport, the temperature had dropped into the teens and four inches of snow had fallen in the small vacation destination overnight.

As the helicopter circled for the landing, visions of a beach with a bright sun, a chaise lounge and a fruity alcoholic drink flirted in Jordon's head. She'd booked a long-awaited vacation in Florida for the end of next week.

Hopefully, this mess in Branson could be cleaned up soon enough that she wouldn't have to postpone the long-awaited vacation.

She was here only in an advisory position as a favor between her FBI director and the Branson mayor. All she knew was that there had been three murders in as many months committed in a popular bed-and-breakfast. The latest murder victim had been stabbed to death and discovered by a maid in her room the day before.

Jordon played nice with others when it was absolutely necessary, but she preferred to work alone. She had a feeling that Director Tom Langford had tapped her for this job, knowing that she would have to try to work with a police chief who probably didn't want her here.

"It builds character to step out of your comfort zone." She wished she had a dime for every time Tom had said that to her in the last couple of years. "Don't be a cowboy, Jordon. That's what nearly got you killed a year ago," he'd reminded her right before she'd left.

The heart-shaped pattern of cigarette-burn scars on her left hip itched as memories of an old cellar and a serial killer named Ralph Hicks flashed in her head.

It had been nearly a year since she'd almost

become the sixth victim of the man who had tortured and killed five other women over a six-month period in the Kansas City area. Thankfully, she had been the one who had walked out of that dank, terrifying cellar and Ralph Hicks had come out in a body bag.

The bump of the helicopter touching down snapped her back to the here and now. Jordon thanked the pilot, grabbed her two bags and climbed down to the tarmac, where a uniformed police officer greeted her.

"Agent James, I'm Lieutenant Mark Johnson." He shouted above the whoop whoop of the helicopter blades as the aircraft took off once again.

He grabbed her bags from her. "Good to have you here. My car is parked over here." He turned and headed for the parking lot in the distance. An icy gust of wind half stole her breath away as she quickly followed behind him.

Within minutes they were in his patrol car with a steady flow of heated air blowing in her face. "Have you been to Branson before?" he asked when they pulled away from the airport.

"Never, although I've certainly heard a lot about it from coworkers who have been here," she replied. She held her hands up to the air vents and squinted against the late-afternoon sunshine that glared off the snow cover.

At least the highway they traveled had been cleared, but as he turned onto a narrow snow-packed street that headed straight downhill, her breath caught in the back of her throat.

They had gone from city highway to thick woods and a precarious country road with a simple right-hand turn. "Diamond Cove is down this way," Mark said. "Chief of Police Gabriel Walters is waiting for you there." He eased up on the gas as the back end of the car slid ominously to the left.

Every muscle in Jordon's body tensed and didn't relax again until they had turned into a driveway in front of a cozy-looking log cabin. He parked next to a police car that was already there and shut off the engine.

"Welcome to Diamond Cove Bed-and-Breakfast," Mark said. "This is the main office and dining area." He pointed to the right. "As you can see through the trees up on the ridge there are four cabins that hold two suites each. The latest victim, Sandy Peters, was found in her bed in unit three yesterday morning by one of the housekeeping staff."

Jordon gazed at the four small log cabins with front porches. With the lack of leaves on the trees they were easily visible. Outside each doorway were two rocking chairs for the guests' pleasure.

In the spring and summer the thick woods that surrounded the cabins would hide them from view. The air would be filled with bird-song and squirrels would provide comic relief with their antics. Those rocking chairs would make perfect perches to nature-watch.

On the surface, the Diamond Cove resort appeared to be nestled on a secluded mountainside and promised peace and seclusion for the city-weary. But the peace had been shattered by three horrendous murders.

Mark opened his car door and Jordon did the same. A gust of frigid air greeted her and snow crunched underfoot as she got out of the car. Once again she thought of the beach and released a frosty, deep sigh.

"Follow me," he said after grabbing her bags from the backseat.

He bypassed the front door and instead led her around the building on a wraparound porch. They passed a beautiful waterfall that was obviously heated as the water trickled merrily over rocks and into a small pond despite the below-freezing temperature.

They entered the building and stepped into the main dining room. The air smelled of a hint of cinnamon, wood smoke and rich, freshly brewed coffee.

It was a small, cozy area with two long tables draped in elegant white cloths. Fat white candles and crystal salt and pepper shakers marked the center of each table. A bookcase holding preserves, jellies and cookbooks for sale was against one wall, and a fireplace with two chairs added to the homey atmosphere.

Jordon took all of this in with a single glance, for it was the man seated in one of the chairs by the fireplace that captured her full attention.

Chief of Police Gabriel Walters held a cup of coffee in his hand and stared into the flames of the crackling fire. He was apparently so deep in thought he hadn't even heard them come in.

His black hair was neatly cut and broad shoulders filled out the dark blue uniform shirt. His profile indicated a strong jawline and a perfectly straight nose.

"Chief?" Mark said hesitantly.

He shot up out of the chair and a touch of annoyance flashed across his handsome features. It was there only a moment and then covered by a smile that warmed Jordon right down to her frozen toes.

He might not mean the smile, but it didn't

matter. He wore the gesture well even though it didn't quite light up the depths of his intense blue eyes.

"Special Agent James…I'm Chief Walters," he said and took her hand for a firm, no-nonsense shake.

"Please, make it Jordon," she replied.

He nodded and released her hand. "Jordon it is. Please, have a seat. Can I get you a cup of coffee?"

"That would be great," she replied. She unzipped her coat, shrugged it off and sat in the chair next to his in front of the fireplace.

He walked over to Mark and spoke so softly to the man that Jordon couldn't hear. Mark nodded a goodbye to Jordon and left the way they had come.

She watched as Gabriel moved over to a small table that held a coffeemaker and all the accoutrements for all tastes. "Cream? Sugar?" he asked.

"Black is fine," she replied. The man was definitely hot. He boasted not only wonderfully broad shoulders, but also slim hips and a stomach that didn't appear to hold an ounce of body fat.

He hadn't offered her the choice of calling him by his given name and that alone told her he might not be happy to see her. She'd seen him for only a minute and already she had him pegged as intense and probably uptight and rigid.

His physical attractiveness definitely stirred a little fire of heat in the pit of her stomach, but if her suspicions about his personality were right, then she had a feeling it wouldn't be long before she might want to pinch his head off. Time would tell.

He held the coffee cup out to her and she took it with a murmured thanks. Then he returned to the chair next to her. "I don't know how much you know about what's going on here."

"No real specifics. I was only told that there have been three murders here, the most recent victim discovered yesterday morning."

He nodded. "Sandy Peters. She was thirty-four years old and a mystery writer. According to the owners of the resort, she came here every year in January to spend a couple of weeks holed up and writing."

"Married? Divorced?"

"Single, and according to everyone I spoke to yesterday who was close to her, she wasn't dating anyone," he replied. "Besides, she was killed in the same manner as the other two victims."

"Stabbed to death," Jordon said.

"That's right. My investigation hasn't turned up anything the three victims have in common other than they were all guests here at Diamond Cove at the time of their deaths. In fact, they were the only guests here at the time when they were killed."

Jordon took a sip of the coffee and leaned back in the chair. The warmth and scent of the fire combined with the deep smooth tone of his voice would make it easy to be lulled into a semicoma if they weren't talking about murder.

She leaned forward and caught a whiff of his pleasant, woodsy-scented cologne. "So, this doesn't sound like it's about any specific victimology, but tell me about the other victims anyway."

"The first one was twenty-five-year-old Samantha Kent. She and her husband had rented a suite just before Thanksgiving to celebrate their first wedding anniversary. She was stabbed to death on a trail near their cabin on a Tuesday morning."

He grimaced and then continued. "The second victim, Rick Sanders, booked a room a week before Christmas. He was found stabbed in the guest shed. Samantha was a schoolteacher from Kansas City. Rick was a restaurant owner from Dallas who had come here to check out some of the local food. Sandy was from St. Louis."

Jordon was impressed by how easily he rattled off the pertinent information of each victim without any notes. It meant he'd embraced the victims. They weren't just dead bodies to him... They were people. She liked that.

She took another sip of her coffee as he continued. "When Samantha was found on the trail, the first person we looked at hard was her husband, Eric. But he had a solid alibi. He'd been here having breakfast with the owners when she was killed and I could find no motive for him wanting her dead."

"What was she doing outside all alone?" Jordon asked, mentally taking notes of all the information he was giving to her.

"She was an amateur photographer...a nature buff, and according to her husband, she'd decided to skip breakfast on that particular morning to take some photographs. She had a quick cup of coffee here with the owners and her husband to start the day and then she left by herself."

"Who found her body?"

"Billy Bond, the groundskeeper. When he found her she was still breathing but unconscious and bleeding out. She died on the way to the hospital. According to the doctor, she had been attacked only minutes before she was discovered."

"So, the killer is probably local and you have no clue as to the motive," Jordon said.

Gabriel's lips thinned slightly. "No clue as to who or why. I guess that's why Mayor Stoddard thought it was important to bring in the big guns."

A small laugh escaped her despite the obvious displeasure on his face. "Don't worry, Chief Walters. This gun doesn't intend to get in your way. You're the big Uzi and I'm just a little backup handgun."

She held back a sigh. She'd been here only half an hour and already the very hot chief of police appeared to be attempting to engage her in a spitting match.

SHE DIDN'T INTEND to get in his way.

But something about FBI Special Agent Jordon James was already under his skin.

As Gabriel led her out of the main cabin and toward the smaller cabins so that she could see each of the crime scenes, his gut twisted tight in frustration.

He hadn't been happy when the mayor had insisted they get help from the FBI, even in just an advisory position. He'd taken it as a vote of no confidence from the man who was his boss.

Jordon James had said nothing out of line. She'd been a complete professional so far, but while they'd talked he'd had some very unprofessional thoughts roll through his head.

She was strikingly pretty with her short curly dark hair and green eyes that sparked not only a keen intelligence, but with what he sensed was also a glimmer of humor.

When she'd shrugged out of her coat it had been impossible not to notice the length of her legs encased in the tight black slacks and the thrust of her full breasts against the white cotton of her blouse. Even the holster around her waist didn't detract from her innate femininity.

He'd been living and breathing murder since the first body had been found here almost three months ago. His instant, sharp physical attraction to Jordon had momentarily shaken him.

He now followed her up the wooden stairs that led to the ridge where the cabins were located. At least out here in the cold air he couldn't smell the enticing flowery perfume that had permeated the air the moment she'd sat next to him in the dining room.

She reached the top of the ridge and turned

back to wait for him. When he joined her he pointed to a small structure just to the right.

"That's the guest shed where Rick Sanders was found." She fell into step next to him as they approached the building where a cheerful hand-painted Welcome sign hung over the door.

They stepped inside to the tinkle of a little bell, and even though he'd been in the shed at least twenty times since the night that Rick's body had been found, his gaze took everything in as if it was the very first time he'd been inside the small building.

A bifold door to the left hid a stackable washer and dryer. A round table and chairs to the right invited the guests to sit and relax. Beyond that was another closed door that led to a small storage room.

A counter held a fancy coffeemaker with a carousel of little flavored coffees, and beneath the counter, a glass-doored refrigerator displayed a variety of sodas and bottled water for the guests to enjoy at no cost.

"What a nice idea for the people staying here," Jordon said.

Gabriel nodded, although his head filled with the vision of Rick Sanders dead on the floor, his back riddled with stab wounds. "He never saw what was coming. It appeared that he was standing in front of the coffeemaker waiting for a hot chocolate when he was attacked from behind."

She looked up at the bell hanging over the doorway. "He didn't hear it coming?"

"The bell wasn't hung there until after his murder," Gabriel explained. He watched Jordon closely as her narrowed gaze once again swept the room. He couldn't help but notice the long length of her dark eyelashes and the slightly pouty fullness of her lips.

She opened the door to the storage room, where Gabriel knew the space held only cases of soda, boxes of the little coffee pods, paper napkins and other supplies.

"Okay," she said and gazed at him with eyes that gave away nothing.

"See anything me and my men might have missed?"

"Yes. In fact, I think I've solved the case. It was Colonel Mustard in the library with a wrench," she replied flippantly. He stared at her in stunned surprise. "Where to next?" she asked before he could even begin to formulate a response.

They exited the guest shed and he led her down a path that would eventually take them to the place where Samantha Kent's body had been found.

"There's about seven acres of trails here," he said.

"Good grief. I hope we aren't walking them all now." She pulled her coat collar closer around her slender neck. "I hate this weather. I've got a date with a beach in Florida at the end of next week and I can't wait to get in a bathing suit and enjoy a fruity, fun alcoholic beverage."

"Then I guess you'll need to hurry to solve this case in time to get to the beach," he replied. He took another couple of steps then halted when he realized she wasn't with him.

He turned around. She stood stock-still, her green eyes narrowed as if he was a puzzling crime scene she was analyzing. "Are you normally a jerk or are you just acting like one especially for me?"

Despite the cold air, a wave of warmth filled his cheeks. "No, I'm not normally a jerk," he replied. He drew in a deep breath and released it slowly. "But I guess I have been acting like one since you arrived and I apologize." He had to admit to himself that he'd been a bit antagonistic with her. It wasn't her fault she was here. She was just doing her job like he was trying to do his.

"Apology accepted," she said easily and

grinned. "Can I expect more jerk from you or are you over it now?"

"I'm not sure," he admitted. He shoved his hands into his coat pockets. "It's not you personally."

Her grin widened. "Trust me, I didn't think it was about me personally. You haven't known me long enough to have attitude with me, although I'm sure if I'm here for a few more days that will eventually come."

He gazed at her curiously. "Why? Are you difficult to work with?"

"I'll let you draw your own conclusions." Her smile fell and she wrapped her arms around her chest. "Look, I get it that you probably aren't happy about FBI presence here. But I am here, and we might as well try to work together to solve these murders. Now, can we get on with this? I'm freezing my tush off."

And a fine tush it was, Gabriel thought as they continued walking on the narrow trail. Within minutes they were at the spot where Samantha Kent's body had been found.

"The trees were still fairly full of leaves when she was killed," he said. "Although you can see the cabins from here now, they weren't visible at the time of the murder."

Once again Jordon silently surveyed the

scene. "She didn't scream or cry out for help? Nobody heard anything?"

"Nobody admitted to hearing anything. She was attacked from behind like Rick. She didn't have a single defensive wound and Billy didn't see or hear anyone else in the woods when he found her." The frustration of the cases burned in his stomach as once again his mind provided a memory of this particular crime scene.

Samantha had already been carried away to the hospital by the time Gabriel had arrived on scene, but her blood had stained the autumn leaves where she had fallen, transforming this piece of beautiful woods to a place of haunting, violent death.

"I've seen enough," Jordon said softly.

They were both silent as he led her to unit number three, where Sandy Peters had been found stabbed in her bed.

"Wow. Nice room," Jordon said after they'd stomped the snow off their boots and stepped inside. They both had donned gloves and bootees, as the room was still officially a crime scene.

"All the rooms are this nice," he replied. He stood by the door as Jordon wandered the area.

A king-size log bed was the center focal

point, along with a stone fireplace and a sunken Jacuzzi tub for two. The bed had been stripped down to the mattress, but Sandy's suitcase was still open on one of the chairs in front of the fireplace, and a thick pink robe still hung on a coat tree next to the dresser.

He'd kept things intact in the room as much as possible for Jordon's perusal, although his men had already taken Sandy's cell phone and computer and the bedclothes into evidence. The room had been gone over with a fine-tooth comb and fingerprinted, so this evening he'd have some of his men clear the rest of Sandy's things from the room.

Jordon disappeared into the adjoining bathroom and then reappeared and stared at the tub, where a little basket held packets of bubble bath and two wineglasses with a bottle of white wine perched on the tile.

"There was obviously not a struggle." It was a statement of fact rather than a question.

"And the door wasn't forced," he replied. "It appears that she opened the door and was immediately stabbed. She fell backward to the bed and the attack continued there. She was stabbed a total of twelve times."

A frown danced across Jordon's features. "Overkill... That indicates a rage."

He nodded. "The same kind of rage was evident with the other two victims, as well."

"And the time of death?"

"The coroner placed it between around midnight and five in the morning," he replied. "Hannah, the owners' fifteen-year-old daughter, saw Sandy leaving the guest shed at around nine in the evening. She had a soda in her hand and told Hannah she planned on being up late working."

"What was Hannah doing out and about at that time of night in this weather?"

"One of her jobs here is to make sure the refrigerator is restocked each evening. She was later than usual that night." He looked toward the window where dusk had moved in. "I've arranged interviews with all the staff here to start in the morning at eight. In the meantime, we should get you settled in for the night. I've made arrangements for you to stay at a motel not far from here."

She looked at him in surprise. "Why would I stay at another motel? I'm assuming there are vacant rooms here?"

"Yes, but there is also a killer using this bed-and-breakfast as his personal playground."

"All the more reason for me to stay here," she replied.

Gabriel frowned. "I really don't like the

idea. I think it would be much better if you stayed somewhere else."

"I'll be fine here. I'm armed and I'm trained. Just get me a key and point me to a room."

The burn in his gut intensified. Even though he barely knew Jordon, he recognized the stubborn upward thrust of a chin, the resolute shine in her eyes.

The killer was savvy enough not to leave any evidence behind. In savagely murdering three people he hadn't made any mistakes that Gabriel had been able to find.

The last thing Gabriel wanted was for FBI Special Agent Jordon James to become the fourth victim.

Chapter Two

When they returned to the main dining room, two adults and two teenagers awaited them. Gabriel introduced them as owners Ted and Joan Overton and their two children, fifteen-year-old Hannah and seventeen-year-old Jason.

"I made fresh coffee and some sandwiches," Joan said as she and her husband jumped up from the table where they'd been seated. She hurried over to stand next to the table with the coffeemaker and twisted her hands together as if unsure what to do next.

"Thank you—I'd love a cup," Jordon said. "And the sandwiches look wonderful." Joan's pretty features lit up as if she was pleased to be able to serve somebody.

"We've canceled all of our reservations for the next two weeks," Ted said. Jordon took a seat across from him and Gabriel sat next to Jason.

"There weren't that many to cancel," Joan said as she set a cup of coffee in front of Jordon and then sat next to her husband. "This is our slowest time of year, but reservations had already fallen off because of the bad publicity we've received. Social media is destroying us."

"Your place is lovely," Jordon said. "How long have you all owned it?"

"We bought it a little over a year ago," Ted said. "We'd talked about leaving the rat race behind and doing something like this for years, and then this place came on the market as a foreclosure and so we bit the bullet and made the move."

"Made the move from where?" Jordon asked. She took half of one of the thick ham-and-cheese sandwiches that were on a platter and placed it on the small plate in front of her.

"Oklahoma City," Ted replied. He was a tall, thin man with dark hair and brown eyes, and his children took after him rather than their shorter, blond-haired, blue-eyed mother.

"Do we need to be here?" Jason asked. His cheeks colored slightly as Jordon turned her gaze on him. "I don't know anything about what's happened around here and I've got homework to finish."

Jordon shifted her gaze to Gabriel, who shrugged. She turned back to Jason. "I don't see any reason for you to hang around here while we talk to your mother and father." The young man was nearly out of his chair before Jordon had finished speaking.

"What about me?" Hannah asked. "I've already told Chief Walters everything I know."

"As long as it's okay with your parents, you both can be excused for tonight," Jordon replied. Hannah also flew out of her chair and pulled a cell phone from her pocket.

"Go directly to the house and no place else," Ted said.

"Where's the house?" Jordon asked as the two teenagers left the building.

"Across the street. It came with this property," Ted replied. "It's a nice three-bedroom with a lake view."

"And it has a huge detached garage that's far enough away from the house that I can't hear the banging and curses or noises that Ted makes when he's working on one of the cars or in the middle of a woodworking project," Joan added.

For the next hour Jordon questioned the

couple about the murders, the victims and the daily operation of the bed-and-breakfast.

Gabriel was mostly silent during the conversation. She was grateful he allowed her to go over information she was certain he already knew.

The body language between the couple indicated a close, loving relationship, and Jordon sensed no underlying tension other than what would be deemed normal under the conditions.

By the time they'd finished up, night had fallen outside. "Agent James would like to stay here," Gabriel said when the interview had wound down. A deep frown cut across his forehead. "That wouldn't be a problem, would it?"

"Of course not," Joan replied with a touch of surprise.

"Are you sure you want to do that?" Ted asked.

"Positive," Jordon replied without hesitation. Gabriel's silent disapproval of the plan wafted in the air, but Jordon's mind was made up.

"We'll put you in unit seven," Ted said. They all got up from the table. "I'll just go get the key for you." He left the dining room through a door that Jordon assumed led into the main office.

"Breakfast is served from seven to nine. If that doesn't work for you just let me know," Joan said. "We'll be glad to do whatever we can to accommodate you while you're here."

"I'd like you to keep things the way you would for any other guest," Jordon replied.

"And I'll be here around seven in the morning so that we can begin interviewing the staff at eight," Gabriel said. "I hope you don't mind me joining Agent James here for breakfast."

"You know you're always welcome here, Chief Walters," Joan said warmly.

Ted returned to the dining room and handed Jordon a room key. "I'll just grab my coat and show you to the room."

"Don't worry about it, Ted. I'll see her to the room," Gabriel replied. He pulled on his coat and Jordon did the same.

"Thank you for the sandwiches. It was very thoughtful of you," Jordon said to Joan.

"It was my pleasure," Joan replied.

"And I won't be needing daily maid service while I'm here. Once a week or so would be fine just for clean towels and sheets, and I can change my own bed."

Joan nodded. "If that's what you want.

Hopefully the case will be solved soon and you won't even be here long enough for that."

"We'll see you in the morning." Gabriel picked up Jordon's suitcases.

Jordon took the smaller of the bags from him. "They seem like a nice couple," she said when they were out of the building and heading up the stairs to the cabins.

"They are. They have good kids, too. Both Jason and Hannah are excellent students and they work here for their parents after school." He shifted the suitcase he carried from one hand to the other. "But these murders are quickly destroying their livelihood."

"So, who would want to do that?" The cold air nearly stole her breath away as they trudged up the stairs to the row of cabins. She sighed in relief as they reached the unit she would call home for the duration of her stay.

"A few people come to mind."

She set the suitcase she carried down and retrieved the room key from her pocket. Although she was intrigued by any suspects he might have in mind, at the moment all she wanted to do was get out of the frigid night air.

She sighed in relief as she stepped into the warm room. Gabriel followed her just inside the door and set her suitcase on the floor. She shrugged out of her coat, flipped the switch that made the flames in the fireplace jump to life and then turned back to look at him. "So who are these people who come to mind?"

"Actually, I'd rather not get into all that tonight. It's getting late and I'll just let you get settled in. Why don't I meet you in the dining room at seven tomorrow morning and we can discuss it more then."

It was only eight o'clock, hardly a late night, but it was obvious by the rigid set of his shoulders and how close he stood to the door that he wasn't comfortable having a long conversation in the intimacy of the room.

Maybe he had a wife to get home to, she thought, although there was no wedding ring on his finger. She pegged him in his midthirties, certainly not only old enough to be married, but also to have some children running around.

"Okay, then I guess I'll see you in the morning," she said. "Oh, and one more thing. If it's possible, I'd like to have a car at my disposal while I'm here."

He gave a curt nod. "I'll see to it that you have one first thing in the morning. And we should exchange cell phone numbers." He pulled his phone from his pocket.

With her number in his phone and his in

hers, Gabriel stared at her for a long moment. "You know I don't approve of you staying here. You need to call me immediately if you feel uncomfortable here or believe you're in any kind of danger."

The only danger at the moment was the possibility of getting lost in the simmering depths of his eyes. She'd watched those blue eyes through the course of the evening. She wondered if he had any idea how expressive they were.

As she'd spoken to the Overtons, his eyes had alternately radiated with a soft sympathy and a deep frustration. It was only when he gazed at her that they became utterly shuttered and unfathomable.

"Jordon?" he said, pulling her from her momentary contemplation.

"Don't worry about me. I'll be just fine." Her hand fell to the butt of her gun to emphasize her point. "Good night, Chief Walters. I'll see you in the morning."

He gave her a curt nod and then left the room. Jordon locked the door behind him. There was no dead bolt, only the simple lock in the doorknob. Apparently security had never been a real issue before the murders. She was vaguely surprised dead bolts hadn't been installed since then.

She sank down on the chair next to the fireplace, her thoughts consumed by the man who had just taken his bedroom eyes and his heady woodsy scent with him.

She had no idea how well they were going to work together. She wasn't sure yet how open he was to hearing anything she might have to say about the cases. But the bottom line was she had a job to do and she would do her best with or without his cooperation.

She pulled herself up off the chair and opened one of the suitcases on the bed. It took her only minutes to unpack and then place her toiletries in the bathroom.

She set up her laptop computer on the small coffee table in front of the fireplace and for the next half hour typed in notes and impressions while things were still fresh in her mind.

By the time she finished, she was still too wound up even to think about going to sleep. She should just pull her nightgown on and go to bed, but she had a feeling she would just stare at the dark ceiling while sleep remained elusive.

Although the idea of going outside in the cold night air was abhorrent, she pulled on her coat and snow boots with the intention of retrieving one of the flavored coffees that tasted like dessert from the guest shed.

The path to the shed was lit by small solar lights in the ground, and despite the frosty air, she kept her coat open and her hand on the butt of her gun. The night was soundless, the eerie quiet that thick snow cover always brought.

All of her senses went on high alert. There was no way she intended to be careless on her first night or any other night she stayed here.

A faint scent of pine lingered in the air and she noticed through the bare trees that the main building was dark. She was all alone on the Diamond Cove grounds.

When she reached the guest shed and stepped inside, a light blinked on and the bell tinkled overhead. She made sure the door was closed firmly behind her and then checked behind the door that hid the washer and dryer to make sure nobody was hiding there. She then moved to the storage room. With her gun in her hand, she threw open the door and breathed a small sigh of relief.

Assured that she was alone, she picked out a chocolate-flavored coffee, placed it in the coffee machine and then faced the door as she waited for the foam cup to fill.

This was what poor Rick Sanders had done. He'd come in here seeking a nice cup of hot chocolate and instead had ended up stabbed viciously in the back.

When the coffeemaker whooshed the last of the liquid into the foam cup, she turned and grabbed it and went back out into the quiet of the night.

She was halfway to her cabin when the center of her back began to burn and she had the wild sense that somebody was watching her.

She whirled around, her sudden movement sloshing hot coffee onto her hand as she gripped the butt of her gun with the other. Nobody. There was nobody on the path behind her.

There was no sound, no sign of anyone sharing the night with her. She hurried the rest of the way to her room, unlocked her door and went back inside. She set her coffee on the low table in front of the fireplace and then moved the curtain at the window aside to peer out.

Despite the fact that she saw nothing to cause her concern, she couldn't shake the feeling that somebody had been out there, somebody who had been watching her…waiting for the perfect opportunity to strike.

GABRIEL WAS UP before dawn, his thoughts shooting a hundred different directions and making any further sleep impossible. He got out of bed, pulled a thick black robe around him and then padded into the kitchen to make coffee.

As it began to brew he took a quick shower, dressed for the day and then sank down at the kitchen table with a cup of hot coffee before him.

He should be thinking about murder. He should be thinking about the interviews he'd set up for the day, but instead his head was filled with questions about the long-legged, green-eyed woman who had blown into his case…into his town on a gust of cold air.

Could she accomplish what he hadn't been able to do? Could she somehow identify the killer, who had remained elusive so far to him, and get him behind bars? If she could, then it would be worth whatever he had to put up with to work with her.

All he wanted was to get this murderer off his streets. He'd never dreamed when he'd left the Chicago Police Department behind three years ago to take this job that he'd be dealing with a serial killer in the town known as America's family destination.

He'd also never imagined he'd be working

for a mayor who was contentious and petulant, a man who was also a pompous ass and passive-aggressive. It was no wonder the last chief of police had quit after only less than a year on the job. More than once throughout the past three years Gabriel had considered walking away from here and starting over someplace else.

Once again his thoughts went to Jordon. There was no question that he found her extremely attractive. He even admired the fact that she'd called him out on the jabs he'd shot at her. But that didn't mean he was going to like her and it certainly didn't mean he was going to work well with her.

She already had one strike against her. He hadn't approved of her decision to stay at Diamond Cove. She'd known he didn't like it and yet she'd done it anyway. She was placing herself in the eye of a storm, and as far as he was concerned, it was an unnecessary, foolish risk.

By the time he finished two cups of coffee and his scattered musings, the morning sun had peeked up over the horizon and it was almost six thirty.

He made a call to arrange for a patrol car to be taken to the bed-and-breakfast for Jordon to use and then pulled on his coat to head out.

It was going to be a long day. Diamond Cove employed four people full-time and he'd arranged for all of them to be interviewed today along with a few others away from the bed-and-breakfast, as well.

As he got into his car he swallowed a sigh of frustration. Everyone they would be interviewing about the latest murder were people he'd interviewed at least twice before with the first two homicides.

He was desperate for some new information that might lead to an arrest, but he really wasn't expecting to get any that day.

Thankfully, the road crews had handled the snowfall well and the streets had been cleared for both the locals and the tourists who braved the winter weather for a vacation.

There was another snowstorm forecast for early next week. Jordon better enjoy the next few days of sunshine because, according to the weather report, the approaching snowstorm was going to be a bad one.

Maybe they'd get lucky and solve the case before the storm hit. She could keep her date with the Florida beach and he could get back to dealing with the usual crimes that always occurred in a tourist town.

He arrived at the bed-and-breakfast at ten till seven and parked next to the patrol car that Jordon would use. He retrieved the keys from under the floor mat and then headed to the dining room.

Jordon was already seated at a table and he didn't like the way his adrenaline jumped up a bit at the sight of her. Once again she was dressed in the black slacks that hugged every curve and a white, tailored blouse—the un-official uniform of FBI agents everywhere.

"Good morning," she said. Her eyes were bright and she exuded the energy of some-body who had slept well and was eager to face a new day.

"Morning," he replied. He took off his coat and slung it over the back of a chair and then got himself a cup of coffee and sat across from her. The scent of fresh spring flowers wafted from her.

"Are you a morning person, Chief Wal-ters?" she asked.

He looked at her in surprise. "I've never thought about it before. Why?"

"My ex-husband wasn't a morning person and he found my cheerful morning chatter particularly irritating. If you need me to keep quiet until you've had a couple of cups of cof-fee, that's information I need to know."

"How long have you been divorced?" he asked curiously.

"Three years. What about you? Married? Divorced? In a relationship?"

"Single," he replied, although he'd always thought that by the time he reached thirty-five years old he'd be happily married with a couple of children. That birthday had passed two months ago and there was no special woman in his life, let alone any children.

"Here are the keys to a patrol car you can use while you're here." He slid the keys across the table.

"Thanks. I appreciate it," she replied.

"Good morning, Chief," Joan said as she came into the room carrying two plates. "We heard you come in and I figured you were both ready for some breakfast."

"Oh my gosh, this is too pretty to eat," Jordon said as she gazed at the huge waffle topped with plump strawberries and a generous dollop of whipped cream.

"Speak for yourself," Gabriel replied as he grabbed one of the pitchers of warm syrup from the center of the table. "As far as I'm concerned, Joan makes the best waffles in town."

"Appreciate it, Chief," Joan replied with a smile of pleasure. She poured herself a cup of coffee and then joined them at the table.

Within minutes Ted also appeared to drink coffee while Gabriel and Jordon ate their meal.

For the next half hour the conversation remained light and pleasant. Ted and Joan told Jordon about the various shows and attractions offered at the many theaters and establishments along the main drag.

"If you have time to do anything, you should go to the Butterfly Palace," Joan said. "It's one of my favorite places here in Branson. It's like walking in an enchanted forest with different species of butterflies everywhere."

"That sounds nice, but I don't plan on having any downtime to enjoy the local flavor while I'm here," Jordon replied. "I've got a vacation planned in Florida next week so I can get away from the cold and the snow."

"So you think you'll be able to have this all solved by the end of next week?" Ted's voice was filled with hope as he looked first at Jordon and then at Gabriel.

The frustration that had been absent while Gabriel had eaten his waffle returned to burn in the pit of his belly. "Unfortunately, I can't promise to solve this case in a timeline that would accommodate Agent James's vacation plans."

"And certainly that isn't what I meant to

imply," Jordon replied with a slight upward thrust to her chin. "Vacation plans can be postponed. I'm committed to being here as long as I need to be in order to be of assistance to Chief Walters." She gave him a decidedly chilly smile.

"And I appreciate any help that I can get," he replied, hoping to diffuse some of the tension that suddenly snapped in the air.

"Speaking of help…" Joan looked out the door where housekeeper Hilary Hollis and her daughter, Ann, stomped their boots before entering the building.

Joan cleared the table and then she and Ted disappeared into the office so Gabriel and Jordon could get down to work.

The interview with the two women didn't take long and Gabriel let Jordon take the lead. It had been twenty-one-year-old Ann who had found Sandy Peters's body when she'd entered the room to clean it.

The young woman's eyes still held the horror of the gruesome discovery as she recounted to Jordon the morning she would never forget.

Jordon took notes on a small pad and handled the interview like the pro she obviously was, not only gaining the information she needed from the two women, but also earning their trust, as well.

"Do you intend for me to conduct all the interviews?" she asked when the women had left and she and Gabriel were alone in the room.

"If you're comfortable with that. I've already spoken to these people several times before with the previous two homicides. Maybe you can get something out of one of them that I couldn't get."

She narrowed her eyes. "Are you being sarcastic?"

He smiled at her ruefully. "No, although I guess I shouldn't be surprised that you think I am." His smile fell into a frown as he continued to gaze at her. "I'm frustrated by these murders. I'm ticked off at the mayor, who has made me feel inadequate since the moment I took this job, and I guess I've been taking all that out on you."

The smile that curved her lips warmed some of the cold places that had resided inside him for months. "Apology accepted," she replied.

"That's twice you've easily accepted an apology from me. Are you always so forgiving?" he asked curiously.

"I try not to sweat the small stuff, although

I have been known to have a temper. Now, who are we seeing next?"

Before he could reply, the outer door swung open and groundskeeper Billy Bond walked in. "I don't know why I've got to be here," Billy said after the introductions had been made and he'd thrown himself into a chair.

He looked at Gabriel, his dark eyes filled with his displeasure. "You've already talked to me a dozen times before when those other two people got killed. I don't know any more now about murder than I did then."

"But I don't know anything about you or anything you've told Chief Walters in the past, so you'll have to humor us and answer some questions for me." Jordon gave the surly man a charming smile. "Why don't we start with you telling me what your duties are around here?"

"I take care of the grounds."

"Can you be a little more specific?"

For the next forty-five minutes Jordon questioned the thirty-two-year-old man who had worked for the bed-and-breakfast since Joan and Ted had opened the doors for business.

Once again admiration for Jordon's interrogation skills filled him as he sipped coffee and listened. And as before as he watched

Billy closely, as he heard what the man had to say, he couldn't help but believe the man was hiding something...but what?

"He's a charming guy," Jordon said wryly when Billy left.

"He definitely lacks some social skills," he replied.

She looked down at her notes. "He answered all of my questions fairly easily, but his posture and facial expressions indicated to me that he wasn't being completely truthful." She looked at Gabriel. "For most of the interview he refused to meet my gaze and I could smell his body sweat. He just seemed a bit shady to me."

"Billy is at the top of my potential suspect list because I have the same concerns about him, but I haven't been able to find anything to tie him to the murders and I can't figure out what he could be lying about."

"He would be on my suspect list simply because he's the one who found Samantha Kent in the woods," she replied. "He could have stabbed her and then waited until he knew she couldn't say anything to identify him and then played the hero in calling for help, knowing that she was going to die before she could say anything to anyone."

He nodded. The same thought had definitely been in his head. "But what's his motive? There's certainly no financial gain in him killing the guests and he doesn't seem to have an ax to grind with the Overtons."

"Crazy doesn't need a rational motive," Jordon replied. Her eyes simmered with what appeared to be a whisper of dark ghosts and Gabriel fought against a sudden dark foreboding of his own.

Chapter Three

It was just before noon when thirty-eight-year-old handyman Ed Rollings sat at the table for his interview. Ed had the face of a cherub, slightly plump and with the open friendliness of a man who'd never met a stranger in his life.

However, the pleasant man was another at the top of Gabriel's list of suspects. Before Ed had arrived, Gabriel had given Jordon just enough information to aid her in her questioning of Ed.

"I understand your brother Kevin owned this place before the Overtons bought it," Jordon now said.

Ed nodded and a strand of his blond hair fell across his broad forehead. "That's right. Kev had big dreams for Diamond Cove but he was short in the financial-planning area." Ed laughed and shook his head. "That's the story of Kevin's life… Big dreams and no smarts for the follow-through."

"And you weren't upset when the Overtons took over here?"

"Why would I be upset? I was just glad they hired me on. I'd been working here when my brother owned it and jobs aren't that easy to find around here. I don't have any hard feelings against Ted and Joan. They didn't screw things up for Kevin. He did that to himself."

"What about your brother? Does he have a grudge against the Overtons?" Jordon asked.

"Kevin has a grudge against the whole world. Most of the time he doesn't even like me or our brother Glen," Ed replied with another laugh.

Gabriel listened to the back and forth and thought about that moment when Jordon's eyes had darkened so much. Although he shouldn't be curious, he was.

He was intrigued about those dark shadows that had momentarily danced in the depths of her eyes. He wondered what had caused her divorce, if her curls were as soft as they looked and what her slightly plump lips might taste like.

He also wondered if the stress of these cases was making him lose his mind. Certainly his thoughts about Jordon were completely inappropriate.

As Jordon continued questioning Ed, Gabriel got up from the table and walked over to stare out the window. From this vantage point he could see not only the cabins up on the ridge, but also the guest shed.

The scene of each murder flashed in his head, along with all of the people he'd interviewed after each one had occurred. Had he interviewed the murderer twice before already? Had he sat across from the person who had viciously stabbed Samantha Kent, Rick Sanders and Sandy Peters and exchanged conversation? Had he somehow missed something vital? That was one of his biggest fears.

"So, where were you on Sunday night when Sandy Peters was killed?" Jordon asked Ed.

Gabriel turned from the window to gaze at the man. "Where I usually am on most nights...at home with my wife."

"And she can corroborate that you didn't leave the house all night?"

Ed laughed yet again. "That woman knows if I turn over in my sleep. She'd definitely know if I left the house, which I didn't." His blue eyes shone with what appeared to be open honesty. "Look, I've got no reason to kill anyone and no reason to hurt Joan and

Ted. Ted pays me a good wage for a day's work. Besides, I don't have it in me to murder somebody."

"I think that's it for now," Jordon said and looked at Gabriel to see if he had anything to add.

"I'm sure Ed will be available if we have any further questions for him," Gabriel said.

"You know where to find me. I'm either here or at home with Millie most of the time," Ed assured them as he got up from the table.

"How do burgers sound for lunch?" Gabriel asked when Ed had left the building.

"Sounds good to me. I'm starving." She got up from the table and reached for her coat slung across the back of her chair.

"I thought we'd grab some lunch and then head into the station. I figured you'd want to look at all the files of the other two murders."

"Definitely," she replied.

It took them only minutes to get into Gabriel's car and he headed for Benny's Burgers, a no-nonsense joint just off the main drag that didn't cater to the tourist trade.

"I seriously doubt that the two housekeepers had anything to do with whatever is going on," she said once they were on their way.

"I agree." The warmth of the heater seemed to intensify the fresh floral scent of her that he found so appealing. He tightened his hands around the steering wheel.

"Tell me more about Ed Rollings and his brothers."

"They were all born and raised here. Ed and his wife have no children but he has two brothers who also live in the area. Glen is two years younger than Ed. He's single and works as a clerk in one of the souvenir shops. And as you now know, his older brother, Kevin, owned Diamond Cove but lost it in bankruptcy."

He pulled into Benny's Burgers' parking lot, pleased to see that the lunch crowd was already gone and only three cars were in the lot.

Within five minutes they had their burgers and were seated across from each other in a booth near the back of the place. At least in here the odors of fried onions and beef were heavy enough to overwhelm Jordon's evocative scent.

"I'm assuming you've interviewed Kevin Rollings," she said and then popped a French fry into her mouth.

"Several times, but not in relationship to Sandy's murder. He's on my list to speak with later this afternoon. He's another one who has been on my short list of suspects."

"You mentioned that Billy Bond was on your list, as well. Anyone else I need to know about?"

He shook his head. "My list is depressingly short and everyone on it has had some sort of an alibi for the first two murders. You can get a better idea of what we've done to investigate those murders when you read the files."

"I'm looking forward to that," she replied.

For the next few minutes they were silent and focused on their meals. The cheeseburger and onion rings were tasteless to Gabriel as thoughts of the three murdered people weighed heavily in his head.

Jordon's appetite didn't appear to suffer at all. She ate her burger and fries, and then, with an assenting nod from him, she pulled his plate closer to her and picked at the onion rings he'd left on his plate.

"This has got to be somebody who wants to hurt Ted and Joan personally," she said.

"I was hesitant to make that call until now." He leaned back against the red leather of the booth. "I've investigated their background thoroughly and so far haven't found anything or anybody that would send up a real red flag."

"What did they do back in Oklahoma City?"

"Ted sold home and vehicle insurance and

Joan was a third-grade teacher. According to all their friends and relatives, they're solid people who didn't have enemies. Their co-workers also spoke highly of them. Kevin Rollings might want to destroy the business just for spite and I can't figure out if Billy Bond is hiding something or not."

"He definitely has a bit of a creep factor going on." She shoved his now-empty plate away.

"Unfortunately, I can't arrest Billy for being a creep and I can't arrest Kevin Rollings on just my suspicion alone. Why did you get a divorce?" The question was out of his mouth before he realized he intended to ask it.

Her eyes widened slightly in surprise and then she smiled. "I was madly in love and got married in an effort to play grown-up and be a traditional kind of woman. It took me two years to realize I wasn't a marriage kind of woman after all." She took a quick sip of her soda, her gaze curious. "What about you? Are you a marriage kind of man?"

"Definitely," he replied firmly.

"Then why aren't you already married? You're a hot-looking guy with a respectable job. Why hasn't some honey already snapped you up?"

"I'm cautious," he admitted. "I want to

make sure that when I finally marry it's a one-shot, forever kind of deal. My parents just celebrated their fortieth anniversary together and I want that kind of a lasting relationship for myself."

"Footloose and fancy-free—that's the life for me," she replied.

The threat of his intense physical attraction to her eased in his mind. She was somebody he would never be interested in pursuing no matter how alluring he found her.

This brief conversation was enough to let him know that he and FBI Special Agent Jordon James wanted very different things in life. He wasn't sure why, but this fact gave him a bit of peace of mind.

For the first time since she'd arrived he relaxed. "I'm glad you're here, Jordon."

"Thanks, Chief Walters. Does that mean lunch is on you?"

He smiled at her. "Yes, lunch is on me, and please call me Gabriel."

The sexy smile she flashed him in return instantly surged an unwanted tension back in his belly.

JORDON STRETCHED WITH her arms overhead and got up from the table. She'd been seated in the small conference room alone for the last couple of hours reading all the information that had been gathered on the murders at the bed-and-breakfast.

She definitely admired how Gabriel and his team had conducted such thorough investigations following each of the crimes. She'd also been aware of the respect shown to Gabriel among everyone in the station.

Nobody had joked or been overly familiar with him, indicating to her that he ran a tight ship and kept himself somewhat distant from his staff. Despite that fact, she'd sensed that he was not only respected, but also well liked.

She paced the length of the table, and her brain whirled with all the information she'd gained in the past three hours of intense study. Still, as thorough as the investigations had been, it was all information that yielded no answer as to who was responsible for the three homicides.

Several times throughout the past couple of hours of being cooped up in the conference room, a female officer named Jane Albright had occasionally popped her head in to see if Jordon needed anything. Only once had Jordon requested a cup of coffee.

The murder crime photos had been utterly gruesome and had built up not only a surge of frustration, but also a rich anger inside her.

She wanted this perp caught before another person was killed and before Joan and Ted Overton were forced to close their doors and lose their livelihood.

She opened the conference room door, stepped out into the short hallway and headed to Gabriel's office. She gave two quick raps on his door, and when she heard his deep voice respond, she walked in.

He looked ridiculously handsome seated behind a large wooden desk, a computer on one side and a stack of files at his right. He started to rise but she waved him back down and sat in a chair opposite the desk.

"Looks like a lot of work," she said and pointed to the files.

"The usual...break-ins, purse-snatchings, robberies and the occasional car theft." He leaned back in the leather chair, his blue eyes gazing at her expectantly.

"If you're waiting for me to give you the name of the killer, don't hold your breath. After reading the files I'm as aggravated as I'm sure you are. This guy is obviously smart and organized. He's not only managed to commit three hideous murders but he's also escaped each scene with nobody seeing him and leaving nothing behind."

He stood. "We can talk about it more on the drive to Mouse's Maze of Mirrors."

A knot spun tight in her chest. "Mouse's Maze of Mirrors?"

He nodded. "It's a fairly new attraction on the strip, and on most afternoons and evenings Kevin Rollings works the door."

She got up from her chair and fought against the unsteady shake of her legs. "I definitely think a chat with Kevin is in order."

Minutes later they were in Gabriel's car and headed to the popular 76 Country Boulevard, where, he explained, most of the theaters, eateries and attractions were located.

As he pointed out places of interest, she tried to still the faint simmer of panic inside her. *See how I got mirrors all set up so you can see yourself? You can watch yourself scream.* Ralph Hicks's gravelly voice filled her head.

The creep had placed three large mirrors in front of all of his victims so they could watch while he tortured them. It had been a horrid form of torture in and of itself.

Buck up, buttercup, she told herself firmly. She'd survived the mirrors and Ralph Hicks. She refused to let those long hours in the cellar affect her now or define who she was. She could deal with a silly maze of mirrors without freaking out.

"I definitely think Kevin Rollings looks good as a potential suspect. His alibis for the other murders weren't exactly stellar," she said, shoving away the haunting memories of her past to focus on the here and now.

"It's tough to break an alibi substantiated by another family member. His brother Glen swore Kevin was at his house drinking and then passed out on his sofa at the time of both the previous murders."

"And of course Glen would have a motive to lie to save his brother's hide," she replied.

"I turned up the heat when I questioned Glen, but he stuck with the story." Gabriel turned into a parking lot in front of a large brown building with a huge picture of a demented-looking mouse painted on the siding. "We'll see what kind of alibi Kevin comes up with for the time of Sandy's murder."

As they got out of the car and approached the building, the sun broke out of the layer of clouds and gleamed on the rich darkness of Gabriel's hair.

He walked with confidence, as if he owned the space around him. Salt of the earth…a traditional man with traditional values and three murders that he was desperate to solve.

He seemed to have taken these crimes personally, otherwise she'd be working with somebody else rather than the chief himself. She hoped together they could get this killer behind bars, where he belonged.

There were no other cars in the lot. There had been few cars on the road. Obviously mid-January after a snowfall was a slow time for the entire town.

They entered into a small lobby with a turnstile and a counter behind which Kevin Rollings sat. Although considerably older than Ed, Kevin had the same blond hair, the same round face as his brother, but that was where the similarities ended.

"I figured you'd be coming to talk to me," he said with a deep scowl that transformed his pleasant features into something mean and ugly.

"You figured right," Gabriel said and then introduced Jordon.

"Got the feds involved in local business." Kevin shook his head and sniffed as if he smelled something dirty.

"Nice to meet you, Kevin. We had a nice chat with your brother Ed early this morning and he had so many wonderful things to say about you." Jordon beamed a smile at the man.

"Ed's a damn fool," Kevin replied. "He's nothing more than a glorified lawn boy."

"What I'd really like to know is where you were on Sunday night," Jordon replied, cutting to the chase.

Kevin smiled, a tight slash of lips that didn't begin to reach his eyes. "That's easy. I met up with a couple of buddies for beers at Hillbilly Harry's. We were there until about midnight and then I went home and crashed out. I've got to admit I was pretty trashed. I could barely stumble from my car to the front door."

"Good thing I didn't meet you on the road. You'd have been looking at a little jail time and a DUI," Gabriel said.

"Kevin, do you live by yourself?" Jordon asked, not wanting the conversation to get off track.

"Yeah. My wife left me two months after the Diamond Cove went into bankruptcy. And yeah, I hold a grudge about the whole thing. If the damned bank would have just given me a little more time, things would have been fine."

His nostrils flared as he continued. "Now I'm working a minimum-wage crap job and barely making ends meet. I don't have anything to do with the Overtons. It's bad enough their kids hang out here with their snot-nosed friends all the time. Do I wish Diamond Cove would fall off the face of the earth? Damn straight. Did I kill those people? Hell, no." He drew in a deep breath and stood from the stool.

"We'll need the names of the men you were with on Sunday night," Jordon said. She was shocked by the venom Kevin hadn't even attempted to hide. He certainly had said enough to keep him high on the suspect list.

"Names?" Gabriel said and pulled a small notebook and pen from his coat pocket.

Kevin heaved a deep, audible sigh. "Glen was there and so was Wesley Mayfield, Tom Richmond, Dave Hampton and Neil Davies. You can check with all of them. They'll tell you I was with them on Sunday night and I wasn't anywhere near Diamond Cove."

"Don't worry. We will check it out." Gabriel tucked the pen and notepad back into his pocket.

"Maybe while you're here do the two of you want to go through the maze? I get a percentage of the till each night and today has definitely been a slow day." The anger that had gripped Kevin's features transformed to a mask of mock pleasantry. "Go see the mouse inside."

"It might be the only fun you'll have while you're here," Gabriel said to Jordon as he pulled his wallet from his pocket.

He paid for their admission and Jordon swallowed against the faint simmer of alarm that attempted to grip her. *It's just a silly tourist attraction*, she told herself. She went through the turnstile with Gabriel just behind her. *Don't freak out. Mirrors can't hurt you.*

A dark corridor led into the maze, where she stepped into a space with five reflections of herself staring back at her. Gabriel was right behind her, a calming presence as the back of her throat threatened to close up.

"This way," he said and led her into a corridor of mirrors to the right.

"Have you been in here before?" she asked.

"No, it's my first time, too." They both jumped as one of the mirrors lit up and displayed an image of the demented mouse and a loud, wicked cackle sounded from overhead.

"If I find you, Mouse, I'll tie your tail into knots," Jordon said as the mirror returned to normal.

"Come on. Let's find our way out of here."

She followed Gabriel's lead through the disorienting corridors as she fought against dark flashbacks. The scars on her hip burned and the phantom scent of cigarette smoke and sizzling flesh filled her nose.

Mouse suddenly appeared behind another mirror. "Beware. If you aren't fast enough I'll pull you into my mouse hole and nobody will ever find you again," a deep voice whispered over the speaker.

Jordon stared at the fat mouse with the oversize teeth and she was back in the cellar clad only in her bra and panties, her arms above her head with her wrists in shackles connected to chains that hung from the low ceiling.

Nobody will ever find you here. You're mine to play with until I get tired of you. Ralph Hicks's voice exploded in her head. *I'm going to take my time and have lots of fun with you, and you get to watch.*

She closed her eyes to dispel the memory and when she opened them again Gabriel was nowhere to be seen. She was alone…with the mirrors, and a deep, gripping panic froze her in place.

Help! Somebody please help me. The pleas filled her head. *Don't let him burn me again. Don't let him do all the things to me that he did to the other women. I don't want to die this way. Please help me!*

"Gabriel?" His name croaked out of the

back of her throat, which had become far too narrow. "Gabriel!" This time the cry was a half scream.

"I'm right here." He appeared next to her.

She grabbed on to his hand and forced a bright smile. "Whew, I thought you were lost." She hoped her voice betrayed none of the sheer panic that had momentarily suffused her.

"I think I found the exit—follow me."

She dropped his hand and practically walked in the backs of his shoes and cracked several bad jokes in an effort to relieve her own tension. After several twists and turns and more warnings from the mouse, they found the door that led outside.

"That was sort of lame," she said as they walked toward his car.

"From what I've heard, this is a really popular attraction among the teenagers in town. And as Kevin said, Jason and Hannah and their friends enjoy it."

"Probably because the girls scream and clutch on to the nearest testosterone-filled boy," she replied drily.

He smiled. "You want to get some dinner before I take you back to your room?"

Knots of tension twisted in her stomach and the taste of panic still filled the back of her throat. "I'm really not that hungry right now. Maybe you could just stop someplace and I'll grab a sandwich to take back to the room for later. I can put it in the mini-fridge until I'm ready to eat."

"There's a sub place not far from here—we can stop there."

They got into the car and Jordon was more than grateful to leave Mouse's Maze of Mirrors behind. She hated her own weakness. She hated that she still felt a bit shaky and dark memories clutched at her heart and invaded her brain.

The last thing she wanted was for Gabriel to sense any weakness in her. "So, what's on the agenda for tomorrow? A roller-coaster ride through a cave? A tour through Ripley's Believe It or Not?" She forced a flippant tone in her voice, determined not to let the memories pull her down.

"Nothing quite so grand. We need to chase down all the men Kevin said he was with Sunday night and confirm his alibi."

"Even if his alibi is confirmed until around midnight, that doesn't clear him for the murder, which took place much later than that," she replied.

"True, but in order to make a solid record, we need to corroborate everything." He pulled into the parking lot of a small place called Subs and Such.

"I'll just run in and grab something," she said. "You want anything?"

"Nah, I'm good. I've got some leftover meat loaf waiting for me at home."

It took her only minutes to get a submarine sandwich, several bags of chips and peanuts and then return to the car. All she wanted now was a long soak in the tub and time to put the mirrors and her memories behind her.

She might not have been woman enough to make her marriage work and she might not have been the daughter her parents wanted her to be, but she was one hell of an FBI agent. That was all she needed to be.

"Do you want me to drive into the station tomorrow morning or are you planning on picking me up?" she asked once they were back in the Diamond Cove parking lot.

"Why don't I come here around seven in the morning to get you? That way I can start the day with one of Joan's breakfasts."

"Sounds good to me." She gathered her purse and the white bag holding her sandwich and snacks. "Then I'll see you in the dining room at seven in the morning."

She gladly escaped the car and stepped into the cold night. She just needed a little time to get herself centered again. The little foray through the maze of mirrors had definitely shaken her up more than she'd expected.

She carried both her purse and her bag of food in her left hand, leaving her right hand to rest on the butt of her gun as she made her way down the path toward her cabin.

The night was once again silent around her and smelled of the clean evergreen that reminded her of Gabriel's attractive woodsy cologne.

She breathed a sigh of relief as she reached her door. She stepped into the warmth of the room and noticed a folded white piece of paper that had apparently been slid beneath the door at some point while she'd been gone.

It was probably something from Joan and Ted, perhaps concerning breakfast the next morning.

She dropped her purse and the sandwich bag on the coffee table and then picked up the paper. She unfolded it and a sizzle of adrenaline whipped through her as she read the message written in red block letters.

U R Next.

Chapter Four

For the first time in months Gabriel's thoughts weren't filled with mayhem and murder. Instead they were filled with a woman who smelled like spring and had almost had a panic attack in a tourist attraction meant to be fun.

She'd played it off well, but he'd picked up on the signs of her distress while they'd gone through the maze. Although she'd made a few jokes, her voice had been slightly higher in pitch and with a hint of breathlessness. When she'd grabbed his hand hers had been icy cold and had trembled. What had caused her such distress?

She was a curious contradiction—tough enough to insist that she stay in a room that might put her at risk as a target for a vicious serial killer, yet shaken up by a silly maze of mirrors. Definitely intriguing.

He turned onto the road that would eventually lead to his house, thoughts of Jordon still taking up all the space in his mind. She was not only beautiful, but also intelligent and with a sense of humor that reminded Gabriel he had a tendency at times to take life and himself a little too seriously.

He'd been sorry that she hadn't been up for dinner with him. Her company was far more appealing than leftover meat loaf and complete solitude.

His cell phone rang. He punched the button on his steering wheel to answer. "Chief Walters," he said.

"Gabriel, can you come back here?" Jordon's voice held a touch of simmering excitement.

"Of course. Is there a problem?"

"Unless I'm the victim of some sort of a sick prank, I think our killer just made contact with me."

Every nerve in his body electrified. "Are you safe?"

"Yes, I'm safe. We'll talk when you get here." She disconnected before he could ask any other questions.

He turned around in the closest driveway and headed back the way he'd come. Adrenaline rushed through him, along with a mix of uneasiness and cautious excitement.

The killer had made contact. What did that mean? His investigation into the other murders hadn't indicated any kind of contact between victim and killer.

He drove as fast as possible and within five minutes was back at the Diamond Cove and out of his car. He hurried toward unit seven, his heartbeat racing.

A rivulet of relief flooded through him when Jordon opened the door to his knock. She'd taken off her coat and boots and appeared to be just fine.

"Thanks for coming back," she said as she closed the door behind him. She pointed to a white piece of paper on the bed. "That was slid beneath my door at some point or another while I was gone today."

He walked over to the bed and stared down at the note. Jordon moved to stand next to him, her fresh scent filling his head as the blatant threat of the words on the paper tightened his gut.

"Do you think it's really from the killer?" she asked. "I didn't see anything in the case files about notes to the victims."

"This is something new and we have to treat it as a serious threat."

"Not that many people know I'm here," she replied.

"This is a small town with a healthy gossip mill. By now probably dozens of people know you're in town and staying here." He turned to look at her. "You need to get out of here. Pack your things and I'll check you into a nearby motel."

She took a step back from him and put her hands on her hips. "I'm not going anywhere." Her eyes flashed and her chin thrust upward. "If that note is from the killer, then it's the first real piece of evidence we have. Hopefully, you can lift a fingerprint off it."

"And it shows that you now have a bull's-eye on your head. I can't allow you in good conscience to remain here." The idea of anything happening to her absolutely horrified him.

She laughed, a low husky sound. "Guess what, Chief Walters—you don't get to allow or not allow me to do anything. You aren't my boss."

He stared back at the note and then looked back at her. "Jordon, be reasonable. You're setting yourself up as bait for somebody who has already killed three people." A new frustration burned in his chest. She was right. He couldn't force her to do anything, but he definitely wanted to change her mind.

"I am being reasonable." She stepped closer to him and placed a hand on his chest. "Gabriel, please don't fight me on this. This is what I'm trained for. This is what I do."

The warmth of her hand seemed to burn right through his coat, through his shirt and into his bare skin. He fought a sudden impulse to grab her in his arms and pull her tight against him.

Crazy. These cases were definitely making him crazy. She dropped her hand back to her side and grinned up at him. "This little gun just might be your best opportunity to catch a killer."

"I would prefer for the little gun to stay safely in a holster," he replied.

"Hey, you made a joke," she said.

He frowned, not comforted by her light tone. This was serious business. "I can't change your mind?" he finally asked.

"No way. I'm a chatty, cheerful morning person and I'm stubborn as hell. Just ask my ex-husband."

He released a deep sigh. "I've got an evidence bag and gloves in my car trunk. I'll just go get them and I'll be right back."

A wealth of worry rode his shoulders as he

headed back outside to his car. There was no question he wanted the killer caught, but not at the expense of Jordon's safety.

She's trained, he told himself. *She's an FBI agent. She knows the risk and obviously embraces it.* But that thought certainly didn't comfort him in any real way.

He grabbed an evidence bag and a pair of gloves from his trunk and then hurried back to the room with a heavy concern still burning inside him.

As he placed the paper in the bag, she sat on the edge of the bed, her eyes glittering brightly. "This is the break you've needed," she said. "I feel it in my bones and my bones rarely lie."

He sealed the bag and then sank down in the chair next to the fireplace, reluctant to leave her alone. "You know I'd feel better if you'd leave here and stay someplace else."

She shook her head. "This is where I need to be. First thing in the morning I'll talk to Ted and Joan and ask them if they saw anyone unusual on the premises today."

He frowned thoughtfully. "Kevin Rollings didn't have time to get here and leave a note after we left the maze."

"That note could have been slipped under my door at any time during the day after we left here. He's not coming off my suspect list so easily and neither are his brothers."

"As far as I'm concerned, all of the Rollings brothers are up there on the list. Before I head home I'll stop at the Overtons' and see if they saw anyone on the property today who shouldn't have been here." He released a deep sigh. "I should put a couple of men on duty here so that you aren't so vulnerable."

"Don't you dare," she replied fervently. "This place is relatively isolated and any men you put here would be visible. Their presence would drive the killer underground. If he doesn't come after me, then he might be patient enough to come after another guest when Joan and Ted open the doors again."

She leaned forward. "You have to trust me, Gabriel. You have to believe that I know the risk and I accept it. He's not going to get the jump on me."

A helpless inevitability swept through him. She was right. The last thing he wanted was for the killer to fall off the radar only to target another guest, and sooner or later, the Overtons would need to open their doors and have paying guests staying here again.

The only thing he could hope was that the note might yield a clue, a fingerprint, an unusual watermark…anything that might lead to the guilty.

"Now, unless you want to watch me slosh around naked in a tub of bubbles and hot water, you'd better get out of here," she said.

His mind was suddenly seized with erotic visions that heated his blood. He consciously willed them away and stood. "I hope whatever you do you'll keep your gun right next to you." He picked up the bagged note from the coffee table.

"Don't look so grim," she said as she got up from the bed. "You need to remember that the other three victims weren't armed and were unaware of the danger that was present here."

There was some comfort. Still, even as she walked him to the door, he realized he'd never been so reluctant to leave a woman. "Stay alert," he said.

"Always. I'll see you in the morning." She opened the door and he walked out into the cold, a cold that couldn't begin to rival the chill in his heart as he thought of Jordon being the next potential victim.

JORDON BOLTED UPRIGHT and grabbed for her gun. She gasped for air as she struggled to leave her nightmares behind. The room was cast in shadows, partially lit by the bathroom light she'd left on all night.

As her breathing returned to normal, she placed her gun back on the nightstand. There was no danger here except for in the dreams she'd left behind.

A glance at the clock on the nightstand let her know it was just after five. It would be another hour before her alarm would ring, but she knew there was no way she'd go back to sleep.

She flopped back on the mattress and stared up at the dark ceiling. It had been months since she'd had any nightmares, but last night her sleep had been filled with them.

Ralph Hicks and his mirrors had invaded her dreams, yanking her back to that cellar and the terror of those long hours. She'd also dreamed of a faceless figure she knew was the killer who had now marked her for death if she was to believe the note left for her.

And there was no reason for her not to believe. Like the other victims, she was the only guest here, and from past actions, that was what the killer liked.

She'd be stupid not to feel a healthy dose of fear, but she knew that specific fear would help her stay alive. She hadn't been afraid on that day a year ago when she'd knocked on

Ralph Hicks's door to ask him some questions about the murders going on in the neighborhood.

The forty-six-year-old man hadn't been on anyone's radar as a suspect, but he had lived next door to the latest victim and so was on the list to be interrogated. She hadn't known she was in danger until he smashed her over the head and rendered her unconscious.

The experience had taught her a valuable lesson, that everyone was a potential suspect and danger could leap out of nowhere. With a sigh she slid out of the bed, grabbed her gun once again and padded into the bathroom to get ready for the day.

As she dressed she thought of the people they'd interviewed the day before. Certainly Kevin Rollings hadn't hidden his resentment of this place, but did that make him their killer? Or was he simply a bitter man who verbally railed against all the perceived injustices of his world? Billy Bond had been sketchy, but that didn't make him a killer, either.

They just didn't have enough information yet. Today they would be pounding the pavement and asking more questions, and hopefully something they stumbled on would help break the case wide open.

She was huddled by the dining room door, freezing her butt off, when Joan unlocked and opened the door at quarter till seven.

"I positively hate winter," she exclaimed as she shrugged off her coat and then headed for the coffee.

"I really don't mind it too much." A frown dug into Joan's forehead and her eyes were dark. "Gabriel told us about the note you got. We didn't see anyone around your door yesterday and we didn't notice any strangers on the property. I wish we would have seen somebody. I can't tell you how much I wish we would have seen the person responsible and you and Chief Walters could make an arrest and end all this."

Jordon poured herself a cup of coffee and then sat at the table and gestured for Joan to join her. "Is running a bed-and-breakfast something you always dreamed about doing?" she asked in an attempt to change the subject and erase Joan's worry at least for a few minutes.

"Always, although it took me some time to get Ted completely on board with the idea. I think he worried that it would be too much work for me, but I absolutely love it. I love that the entire family is involved, and I was ready to get the kids out of the city and into a more family-oriented environment."

"Were you having problems with the children?" Jordon asked curiously.

"No real problems, although Jason had started hanging out with some kids I didn't really approve of and his grades were dropping and Hannah had started getting attitude."

Jordon smiled. "What fifteen-year-old girl doesn't have a little attitude with her mother?"

Joan laughed, but the laughter was short-lived and once again her eyes darkened. "We took such a gamble by making the move here. We put our entire life savings into buying this place. If it doesn't work out for us I don't know what we'll do."

"We're going to get this person, Joan. We're going to get him, and all of your rooms will fill up once again and you all will be just fine."

Joan gave her a grateful smile. "Chief Walters has been wonderful through all of this. He's been working so hard and I know these murders are eating him alive. I'm glad you're here to help him."

"We're definitely doing everything we can," Jordon replied.

Joan leaned back in her chair. "I'm just

sorry you aren't going to get a chance to see some of the sights and have some fun while you're here."

"Actually, I did manage to go through Mouse's Maze of Mirrors."

"Hannah and Jason love that place," Joan replied.

"I wasn't a big fan," Jordon admitted.

"Really? Why not?"

"I don't like mirrors, but that's another story altogether."

Both women turned toward the door as Gabriel came inside. "Good morning," he said.

"Back at you," Jordon replied.

Joan got up from the table. "I'll just go see to breakfast." As Joan left the room, Gabriel took off his coat and sat across from Jordon.

His gaze was dark and intense. "You doing okay?"

"I'm fine as a fiddle."

"No problems overnight?" he asked.

"None at all. Do you know it takes more muscles to frown than it does to smile?"

He sat back in the chair and a smile curved his lips. "Is that better?"

It wasn't just better—it was freaking amazing. He had a smile that could light up the darkest corner of the earth. There was no question that she was intensely attracted to him and she thought he might be more than a little bit drawn to her.

But she also had a feeling Gabriel wasn't interested in a hot sexual fling, and that was all it would be. That was all she would ever be to any man. That was her choice.

For the next fifteen minutes they drank coffee and talked about the plans for the day. Joan brought in plates of biscuits and gravy with sausage patties on the side and a fresh fruit salad. Ted came in and joined them for small talk while they ate.

It was just after eight thirty before they were in Gabriel's car and headed to their first stop for the day to check Kevin's alibi for the night Sandy Peters had been murdered.

"Dave Hampton and I have a bit of a history," Gabriel said. "I've had to arrest him several times for drunk and disorderly. The man loves his booze, and when he drinks too much, he gets stupid and nasty."

"Are you expecting trouble with him? Because if you are, I've got your back, partner."

He cast her a quick glance. "Are you always so sure of yourself?" he asked wryly.

"Only when I'm on the job," she replied. "I know what I'm good at."

"And what are you good at besides being a kick-ass FBI agent?"

Not much. She shoved the two hurtful words away. "I'm great at zapping food in a microwave. I can do five cartwheels in a row without getting dizzy, and when I sing I can make every dog in a five-mile area howl."

He cast her a charming grin. "I'm impressed."

"What about you? Besides being a kick-ass chief of police, what else are you good at?"

He frowned thoughtfully and then the frown lifted, and when he shot her a quick glance, his eyes were a lighter, more inviting blue that she hadn't seen before.

"I can twist an aluminum can into a work of art. I can get almost any dog to eat out of my hand if I'm holding a good piece of steak, and I know all the lyrics to Manfred Mann's 'Blinded by the Light.'"

"Whew, now I'm the one impressed." What impressed her more than anything was that he had responded with the same silly lightness as her. She didn't think he had it in him. There was nothing sexier than a man who didn't always take himself and the world too seriously.

However, the light mood disappeared as he pulled into Charlie's Brake and Muffler Repair. "Dave works here as a mechanic," he said.

"Let's go talk to Dave the drunk and see if he can corroborate Kevin's alibi."

Gray clouds hung low in the sky as they walked toward the large building with four bays. Men's voices rang out along with the sound of noisy tools being used.

They entered into a small office where a man stood behind a counter. "Charlie," Gabriel greeted the man. "How's business?"

"A little slow, but not too bad." His gaze swept the length of Jordon. "I'm hoping you're here because you or the little lady needs a brake job."

"This *little lady* doesn't need brakes," Jordon said drily.

"Actually, we're here to speak to Dave," Gabriel said.

Charlie frowned. "Good grief. What has he done now?"

"Nothing. We just need to ask him a couple of questions," Gabriel replied.

Charlie pointed to a nearby door. "You can use the break room. I'll go get Dave and send him in."

The break room held a card table that cast slightly to one side and was littered with what appeared to be petrified crumbs from meals past, a couple of chairs and a soda machine.

The air smelled of grease and oil. Neither of them sat.

Dave Hampton was a big man with a shock of thick dark hair and a scowl that appeared to have been etched permanently into his face. "I haven't done anything wrong. What's this all about?" He glared first at Gabriel and then at Jordon as he wiped his hands on a filthy rag.

"We just need to ask you a couple of questions and then we'll let you get back to work," Gabriel said.

"Questions about what?" He stuffed the rag into his coverall's pocket.

"About last Sunday night," Gabriel said.

Dave narrowed his eyes. "What about it? I didn't do anything stupid. If somebody said I did then they're a damned liar."

"It's nothing like that," Gabriel assured him. "We just need to know where you were and who you were with."

"A bunch of us went to Hillbilly Harry's to shoot some pool and have a few beers." Dave visibly relaxed.

"Who was with you?"

"Wesley Mayfield, Neil Davies, Tom Richmond and Kevin and Glen Rollings. Is this about that woman's murder?"

"What time did you all leave the bar?" Gabriel asked, ignoring Dave's question.

"I guess it was around midnight or so."

"And none of you left early?"

Dave rocked back on his heels and smiled slyly. "It's Kevin, isn't it? You're wondering if he killed that woman." Dave shook his head and released a small laugh. "Those Rollings boys are thick as thieves, and Kevin hates anything and anyone that has to do with Diamond Cove."

"I got the impression that Kevin didn't get along well with his brothers." Jordon spoke up for the first time.

"That's definitely not true. Kevin raised Glen and Ed after their mother died," Dave said. "According to what Kevin told me, their father was a no-account drunk and Kevin had to step up to be both mother and father to his younger brothers. Like I said before, those three are thick as thieves."

"Was Kevin drunk when you all left the bar?" Jordon asked.

Dave frowned. "We were all a little toasted, but he was no drunker than the rest of us. Is that all? I really need to get back to the shop."

"That's it for now," Gabriel replied.

She and Gabriel didn't speak again until they were back in his car. "There's definitely no honor among thieves," he said as he started the car. "Dave threw Kevin under the bus pretty quickly."

"Kevin told us he got completely trashed, but Dave didn't indicate that Kevin was all that drunk," Jordon replied.

"He was sober enough to drive himself home," Gabriel said. "And Ed has always given me the impression that Kevin isn't close to him or Glen."

Jordon pulled her collar up more tightly around her neck as a cold wind of uneasiness blew through her. "What worries me now is the possibility that we aren't looking for just one killer, but maybe we have a brotherhood of murderers, and that's definitely only going to complicate things."

Chapter Five

"Where to now, boss?" Jordon asked as they pulled back on the main road.

"How do you feel about a little shopping?"

"Like any reasonable woman, I'm always up for some retail therapy," she replied.

"In the store we're going to you can buy a Branson T-shirt or a corncob pipe, a refrigerator magnet or any one of a thousand other items."

"And I'm guessing that Glen Rollings might be my personal shopper?"

He flashed her a quick smile. "Glen is definitely the charmer of the Rollings boys, but I doubt that you need a personal shopper. You strike me as the kind of woman who usually knows exactly what she wants and you don't stop until you get it."

"You've got that right." She turned her head to look out of the passenger window. At the moment she'd like Gabriel Walters's very kissable mouth to be on hers.

The errant thought could only be because she was cold and she knew being in his arms and kissing him would warm her. She'd been cold since she'd arrived in Branson, if not because of the wintry weather, then from the chill of hunting down a cold-blooded serial killer.

Were they up against a single murderer or was it a tag-team effort? Were Glen and Ed helping the brother who raised them get his revenge on Diamond Cove? It was crazy to think somebody would go to such lengths to destroy a business, but revenge killings had happened for far less.

She turned back to look at Gabriel once again. "What I don't understand is if Kevin really wants to destroy Diamond Cove then why not just set fire to the place? Why not build a bomb and blow it all up?"

He turned into the parking lot of the Ozark Shed of Souvenirs and released a deep sigh. "I don't know. I haven't been able to get a handle on this from the very beginning. This is far more evil than a fire or a bomb. It takes a special kind of killer to stab somebody. This person apparently likes to kill up close and personal."

With his words ringing in her ears, they exited the car and headed for the huge shop.

Evil. The word echoed in her brain. Yes, whatever was going on here was definitely evil.

She knew all about evil. She'd been locked in a cellar with evil personified for hours, just praying for death to take her quickly.

She shoved the thought away when they entered the store. She gazed around in amazement. Never had she seen so much stuff in one place. Tote bags and camping lanterns, wooden signs and toilet-paper holders in the shape of outhouses fought shelf space with traveler-size toothpaste and T-shirts and blinged-out wallets and purses.

She followed Gabriel to a sales counter where a gray-haired woman greeted them. "Gabriel," she said with a big smile that lifted all of her wrinkles upward. "I hope that's a girlfriend with you and you've come in to buy one of our real, stunning Ozark gold rings."

Gabriel laughed, a low, deep and appealing sound. "Special Agent James, meet Wanda Tompkins, the orneriest woman in the entire town."

"Nice to meet you, ma'am," Jordon said.

"You, too," Wanda replied and looked back

at Gabriel. "So, if this pretty woman isn't your girlfriend and you aren't here to buy anything, then what can I help you with?"

"We need to speak with Glen," Gabriel said.

"He's upstairs in the back room." Wanda gave Jordon a sly smile. "A shame you aren't his girlfriend. He's a good man who needs a good woman."

"Be careful or I'll arrest you for attempted matchmaking," he replied in a mock-stern voice. "And do I need to remind you that this isn't your first offense."

Wanda laughed and waved a hand at him. "Go on with your bad self." She turned her attention to a group of tourists who had entered the store.

"So Wanda has tried to hook you up?" Jordon asked as they climbed a narrow set of wooden stairs to the second floor.

"When I first arrived in town this store was robbed and that's when I first met Wanda. There was about six months after that when she made finding me a wife her life's mission. She still calls me occasionally to tell me about some nice woman I should meet."

"And did you ever meet any of them?" she asked.

"A few."

"They weren't wife material?"

"They were for somebody, but just not for me."

They reached the top of the stairs and she followed behind him as they wound through several aisles of merchandise. The man was drop-dead gorgeous, wore a respected uniform and seemed to be a genuinely nice guy.

There must be plenty of women in this town who would love to get hitched to a man like him. Cautious, that was what he'd told her he was, but she wondered if maybe he wasn't just super picky.

Jordon had believed she'd married a man like Gabriel, a man who was well respected, principled and moral. She'd been head over heels in love with Jack and after that debacle she never wanted to give any man her heart. Although something about Gabriel made her think some time in a bed with him would be totally awesome.

As they reached the doorway to a storage room, she mentally kicked herself for her errant thoughts. She wasn't here to have a quick, hot hookup. They had a killer to catch.

Like his brothers, Glen Rollings had pleasant features, blond hair and light blue eyes. He was tall and thin, and when Gabriel made the introductions, Glen's gaze swept the length of her.

"You're an FBI agent? Wow. That's hot." He gave her a wink that she assumed he thought was sexy. It was totally lame.

"We want to ask you a few questions," Gabriel said.

Glen gazed at Jordon once again. "Maybe the superhot FBI agent wants to tie me up to interrogate me." He winked at her again.

"Knock it off, Romeo. We're here on serious business," she said with narrowed eyes.

The smile on his face slowly faded. "I know why you're here. Everyone knows a woman was murdered at Diamond Cove." He shook his head. "I wish my brother had never bought that damned place and I also wish he'd keep his mouth shut about how much he hates it."

"So where were you last Sunday night?" Gabriel asked.

As Glen told the same story that Dave had told them earlier, Jordon listened carefully for any inconsistencies.

"And what did you do after you left the bar?" she asked when he was finished.

"Went home...unfortunately alone," he replied.

"Did any neighbors see you? Anyone call you?" she pressed.

"My closest neighbors are a retired couple who go to bed at the crack of dusk, and no, I didn't get any calls." Glen frowned and gazed at Gabriel. "I told you the last time you talked to me that you're barking up the wrong tree. I'm a lover, not a killer."

"Do you text?" Jordon asked.

Glen's frown deepened. "Occasionally. Why?"

"Just curious. Can I see your phone?" Jordon asked.

Glen cast her a sly look. "I may be a dumb country hick, but I've watched enough cop shows to know you need a warrant for that."

Jordon wasn't surprised that he didn't hand it over. Cell phones were as intimate as underwear. You could tell a lot about a person just by looking at their text messages.

Their questioning ended and they headed back downstairs. "I can't leave here without buying a Branson T-shirt," she said. "I love sleeping in oversize T-shirts."

It took her only minutes to find a hot-pink shirt with *Branson* written in bold black letters across the chest. She paid Wanda and then they returned to the car.

They managed to hunt down two more of the men who had been at Hillbilly Harry's with Kevin and Glen on the night of the murder, and then at six thirty they stopped in a pizza place for dinner.

"So, we know Kevin and Glen have a solid alibi until midnight on the night Sandy was murdered," Jordon said as she pulled a piece of the pie onto the smaller plate in front of her.

"But none of the Rollingses can prove that they were home all night after midnight except Ed, who was supposedly home with his wife." He frowned. "We need to touch base with her."

"Could you prove where you were on a specific night between midnight and five or six in the morning?" She didn't wait for his reply. "Unless you have somebody in bed with you, it's hard to have an alibi for that time."

"It's a good thing I don't need to provide an alibi for the middle of the night." He took a bite of the pizza and stared off into the distance.

A lonely man. He wore his loneliness in quiet moments. She recognized it. She understood it because she had a same core of emptiness inside her. She'd had it before her marriage and even more so since the day she'd walked out on her husband. It was a part of her that she tried not to acknowledge.

"I love pepperoni," she said to break the

silence that had stretched too long between them. She picked a piece of it off her pizza slice and popped it into her mouth. "Thick crust and pepperoni—there's nothing better."

For the next ten minutes they talked about the merits of different kinds of pizza. It was a welcome respite after the murder talk that had been the subject of most of their conversations during the day.

It was almost eight when he pulled up in the Diamond Cove parking area. The sun had gone down and dusk had given way to night.

"See you for breakfast?" She grabbed her purse and her shopping bag with the T-shirt.

"I'll be here. Stay safe through the night."

"Stop worrying about me. I'll be just fine," she replied. She got out of the car and opened her coat so she had easy access to her gun.

As she walked to her room, the loneliness she'd sensed in Gabriel resonated deep inside her. There were moments when she wished she had somebody meaningful in her life, somebody to share the ups and downs of the days and hold her in big strong arms through the night.

At one time she'd wanted that, she'd believed she deserved that, but she no longer believed.

"Been there, done that," she muttered as

she unlocked her door and went inside. And it had been a heartbreaking experience that she never wanted to repeat.

She tossed her purse on the bed and pulled the T-shirt out of the shopping bag and carried it and her gun with her into the bathroom.

After a quick shower she pulled on the soft cotton shirt and then climbed into the comfortable big bed with her laptop. As she had before, she typed notes into a growing file she'd named Means and Motive.

It was often those two elements that ultimately solved a case. Who had the means to execute the crime and who had the motive?

She'd been typing in notes for about half an hour when a bump sounded against the building near her door. Every nerve inside her electrified. Her heartbeat raced as she grabbed her gun from the nightstand.

U R Next.

The words screamed inside her head as she slid out of bed and approached the door. If she opened it, would she be met by somebody wielding a deadly sharp knife, ready to follow through on the threat? Was this potentially an attack like the one that had taken Sandy Peters's life?

She gripped her gun more firmly. She wasn't

Sandy Peters and nobody was going to take her by surprise. Drawing a deep breath to steady herself, she reached out, turned the lock and then jerked open the door.

She was greeted only by a cold gust of wind that momentarily stole her breath away. No knife-wielding maniac, no quick attack.

Nobody.

She took a step outside onto the porch and looked around. Nothing. She wouldn't see anyone in the area. The darkness of night would cover anyone's presence.

It was only when she turned to go back into the room that she noticed one of the rocking chairs in front of her window had been moved.

It looked as if somebody had been trying to peer into her window and had accidentally bumped into the chair. Whoever it was, there was definitely no sign of the person now.

She stepped back into the room and closed and locked her door. Her heart still raced as she climbed back into the bed and pointed her gun toward the door.

"Come and get me, you creep," she whispered.

THE NEXT FOUR days passed far too quickly. Jordon had told Gabriel about the Peeping

Tom incident and again he'd tried to get her to move to another motel, but she was adamant that she was right where she wanted... where she needed to be.

She'd been right. She was definitely stubborn and he'd tried a dozen ways to change her mind, but she wasn't budging. The fact that she'd been warned that she was the next victim and she continued staying at Diamond Cove had given him several nightmares over the last couple of nights.

They had interviewed all the men who had been at Hillbilly Harry's on the night of Sandy's murder, they'd pored over the files in an effort to find something they might have missed, and by late Sunday afternoon, Gabriel had all kinds of anxiety burning in the pit of his stomach. He figured by the time these cases were solved he'd have ulcers as big as the Ozark foothills.

The Rollings brothers remained high on the suspect list, along with Billy Bond, who as groundskeeper had easy access to all the victims and might have known their routines, but no new evidence had been revealed to make an arrest.

Unfortunately, the note that had been left for Jordon had yielded nothing...no fingerprints and no distinctive features. The paper was ordinary copy paper that could be bought almost anywhere in town and beyond.

Because it had been written like somebody would write a text, they had questioned everyone again about texting, including Jason and Hannah Overton, who might have thought leaving such a note would be funny.

The two teenagers had proclaimed their innocence passionately and Gabriel had been surprised to learn that almost everyone these days texted in abbreviated language. It had made him feel like an ancient old man.

He now closed the file that held the crime-scene photos and looked across the conference table where Jordon had been reading through the interviews they'd conducted over the last several days.

"Why don't we knock off early, and instead of grabbing a burger out somewhere, I'll take you to my place and fix us a home-cooked meal," he said.

"That sounds absolutely marvelous," she replied. Her eyes were a warm green as she rose from the table and reached for her coat. "A little break will be nice. I've been thinking about murder for the past week."

"Then let's make a pact that for the next couple of hours we won't talk about work at all."

"That's a deal," she instantly agreed.

Within fifteen minutes they were in Gabriel's car and headed to his house. Although he'd certainly had his head immersed in these cases for the last seven days, he'd also had far too many inappropriate thoughts about his "partner."

Her scent invaded his senses when he was sleeping; the visions of her clad only in bubbles in the oversize tub haunted his dreams. He could easily imagine her in bed and clad only in the hot-pink oversize T-shirt she'd bought.

He had no idea if taking her to his house for a meal was a good idea or not, but he did know they both needed a break from the mind-numbing routine of the investigation and the endless fast food they'd eaten over the past week.

"It doesn't look like you're going to make that beach in Florida unless we get a break pretty fast," he said.

"I already canceled my reservations. I also heard on the weather last night that we're supposed to get a big snowstorm here starting tomorrow night." She leaned forward and adjusted the heater vents as if just thinking about the upcoming snow made her cold.

"I'm sorry about your vacation plans."

She leaned back in the seat again. "The

beach will still be there after we catch this creep. What's for dinner?"

"How does spaghetti with meat sauce sound?"

"Fantastic. Do you like to cook?"

"I do. I find it a good stress reliever." He shot her a quick glance. "What do you do to relieve stress?"

"I've always thought primal screaming sounded like a great idea but it's hard to find an empty forest when you need one," she said jokingly. "Actually, stress rolls off my back pretty easily."

"I've noticed that about you." He'd definitely noticed that she used humor to ease tension and alleviate any stress that might be in the air. He wondered what might lurk beneath her humor. What depths of emotions, if any, did she mask with laughter?

And then he wondered why he cared. She was here only temporarily. Despite his visceral attraction to her, there was no way he intended to pursue anything remotely romantic with her.

"Nice place," she said as he pulled up in front of the three-bedroom house he called home. It was a neat place painted a dark brown and flanked by two tall, beautiful evergreen trees.

Still, the Christmas tree lights remained hung and an inflatable Santa had lost his wave as the air had seeped out. He'd had more important things on his mind than taking down Christmas decorations.

"Santa looks pretty sad," she said as they walked up to the front door.

"Yeah, it was a pretty grim Christmas," he replied.

"Have you been here long?" she asked.

"It's a rental but I've been here for the last three years, ever since I moved here from Chicago." He unlocked the front door and ushered her inside.

They entered into the large living room with the open kitchen to the right. "Make yourself at home," he said as he hung his coat in the closet and then did the same with hers.

She walked around the room, her eyes narrowed as they had been when she'd looked at the crime scenes. He looked around the space in an effort to see it through her eyes.

The overstuffed gray sofa was comfortable for sitting and watching the flat-screen television on the opposite wall. The black coffee table held only a small fake flower arrangement that a woman he'd briefly dated had given him. Lamps were on each of the end tables.

She looked at him and smiled. "Your living space is exactly what I expected it to be."

He raised an eyebrow. "What does that mean?"

"It's neat and uncomplicated. A place for everything and everything in its place." She released a short laugh. "You'd go stark raving mad if we lived together."

"You're messy?"

"I like to call it controlled chaos," she replied.

"Interesting," he said. "How about you bring your controlled chaos into the kitchen so I can start working on the meal."

"Sounds like a plan."

Fifteen minutes later he had a pot of seasoned tomato sauce simmering on one burner and stirred a skillet of frying hamburger, garlic and onions on another.

Jordon sat at the table with a beer and filled what was normally the silent hours he'd grown accustomed to with cheerful chatter that he welcomed.

She was so bright and witty and he was vaguely surprised to realize how much he enjoyed her company. Within thirty minutes he learned that she loved old rock and roll, Chinese food and her neighbor's Yorkie named Taz. She loved to dance in her underwear in her living room and preferred white cheddar to yellow.

As they ate the salad, garlic bread and spaghetti, they argued politics and discovered they watched the same television shows and had read many of the same books.

She asked him about his time working in Chicago and he related many of the cases he'd worked on there. She helped clean up the dishes and they settled side by side on the sofa for coffee.

"I needed this," she said as she eased back against the gray cushion.

"The coffee?"

"No, silly man. I needed this break away from thinking about serial killers and the potential demise of Diamond Cove."

He smiled at her. "Nobody has ever had the nerve to call me a silly man before."

She gave him a brash grin. "I call 'em like I see them, cupcake."

He laughed. "I needed this, too. Maybe after this little break we'll approach everything with fresh eyes tomorrow."

"What we need is fresh evidence, and until this creep makes another move, we're in a holding pattern." A frown danced across her forehead as she lifted her coffee cup to her lips.

"And we're doing exactly what we said we wouldn't do by talking about the case."

She took another sip of the coffee and nodded her head. "You're right. So, tell me, Gabriel Walters, what is your deepest fear?"

She constantly surprised him. A long look at her features let him know the question was serious. He feared being alone for the rest of his life. He feared that he would never have the family he desperately wanted, but those were things he didn't share with anyone.

"I'd say my biggest fear right now is that we won't catch this guy and somebody else will wind up dead." He couldn't tell her that he worried that particular somebody would be her. "What about you? What's your deepest fear?"

"Big hairy spiders, especially the jumping kind," she replied flippantly.

He gazed at her for a long moment. "Are you ever serious?"

"I'm serious about getting bad guys off the streets," she replied with a slight upward thrust of her chin.

God, she looked so beautiful with that spark of defiance in her eyes. She intrigued him like no other woman had ever done before.

Despite their long hours of working together over the last week, in spite of all the conversations they'd shared, he felt like he'd just scratched the surface of her. He shouldn't want to go any deeper. A superficial relationship was all he needed for them to work well together.

However, right at this moment with her scent wafting in the air and her eyes the soft green of a beautiful spring day, he wanted more. "Tell me why you're afraid of mirrors," he said.

Her eyes instantly darkened and her chin shot up once again. "What makes you think I'm afraid of mirrors?"

He held her gaze intently. A faint color danced into her cheeks. She set her coffee cup on the table in front of them and wrapped her arms around herself. She shifted her gaze to someplace in the distance just behind him and released a shuddery sigh.

"His name was Ralph Hicks." Her voice was soft and her eyes remained shadowed. "He had already tortured and killed five women before I knocked on his door to interview him. I was officially off duty for the day, but I decided to go ahead and get the interview done on my way home from work." She shook her head and her face paled. "I should have gone straight home and danced in my underwear."

He fought the impulse to move closer to her. She looked small and achingly vulnerable as she pressed herself farther into the corner of the sofa.

She drew in a deep breath and continued. "He was so pleasant and unassuming-looking. He invited me inside and nothing rang a bell of alarm in my head. I stepped in and he bashed me over the head with a small bat. I never saw it coming."

She unwound her arms and leaned forward to grab her coffee cup, but before she did, he reached out and took her hand in his. Icy cold and so achingly small. She wound her fingers with his and he slid closer to her. Her face had paled to an unnatural white and her lower lip trembled for just a moment.

"I'm sorry I asked," he said regretfully.

"It's okay." She gave him a small smile that did nothing to light up her eyes. "Thankfully, after he hit me, the last thing I did before I passed out was slide my cell phone under his sofa. When I regained consciousness I was in my underwear and strung up with chains and there were three floor-length mirrors in front of me. Ralph liked his victims to watch themselves as he tortured them."

Gabriel tightened his hand around hers, his stomach churning with sickness as he could only imagine the horrors she had endured. He wanted to rescue her from her past, from that horror, something that he knew wasn't possible.

"I was lucky. By the time he had me trussed up, he decided it was his bedtime. I didn't see him again until midmorning the next day. By the time he came down the stairs to have his fun with me, my fellow agents already knew I was in trouble because I hadn't shown up for work and I never, ever missed work."

"They traced your phone," he said.

She nodded. "They came in hard and fast, but not before Ralph had played on my hip with a lit cigarette." She released his hand and leaned back once again. "The good news is Ralph got a bullet in his chest and I walked out of there with just a heart-shaped scar."

"And an aversion to mirrors," he added.

"Only if there's more than one," she replied as her face regained most of its color. "And now I think it's time you get me back to Diamond Cove."

He wanted to protest. He wanted more time with her, but her eyes remained hollow and he realized that sharing her story had taken an emotional toll on her.

Twenty minutes later they were back at the bed-and-breakfast and Gabriel got out of the car as she did. "What are you doing?" she asked.

"I just thought I'd walk you to your door," he replied. She'd been quiet on the way back and he'd cursed himself for digging deep enough to dredge up what must have been horrendous memories for her. If he had any questions about whether there was something behind her humor and laughter, he now had the answer.

"That isn't necessary," she protested.

"I know, but it's something I feel like doing. Besides, if the weather forecast is right, by Tuesday morning I might not be able to make it here at all." He walked behind her on the small path.

"Ugh, don't remind me. More snow, more winter—it makes me want to throw up," she replied.

They reached her door and she turned to face him. Her features were softly lit by the nearby solar lamps. "Thank you for the meal and the conversation."

"I'm sorry some of the conversation was difficult for you."

She smiled up at him. "It's something that happened to me, but it's in the past and I survived." Her gaze softened. "When I first arrived here I was sure you were going to be an inflexible, boneheaded pain in my butt, but I was wrong about you. Thank you for putting up with me, Gabriel."

He watched her lips moving, and before he realized his intent, he covered her mouth with his. The evening air was cold, but her lips were wonderfully hot and inviting.

She opened her mouth to him, welcoming him as his tongue deepened the kiss. White-hot desire seared through him. All rational thought momentarily left him, and it wasn't until she raised a hand to gently touch his cheek that rational thought slammed back into his head.

He broke the kiss and stepped back from her, appalled by what he'd just done. It had been a total lack of control. "I'm sorry. That was completely unprofessional and wrong."

"It sure didn't feel wrong," she replied, her cheeks flushed with a becoming pink.

He took another step backward. "Still, it won't happen again."

"Don't bet on it." She dug her key out of her purse and then smiled at him. "Good night, Gabriel. I'll see you in the morning." She opened her door and disappeared inside.

He stared at her closed door for a long moment as he waited for the desire inside him to ebb. Finally, with the frigid night air seeping into his bones, he turned and hurried to his car.

Jordon James was like no other woman he had ever dated. *She's a partner, not a date*, he reminded himself firmly as he started his engine and pulled out of the Diamond Cove parking lot.

They needed to get this case solved sooner rather than later. They needed to find the murderer so Jordon could get back to Kansas City before he really did something boneheaded.

Chapter Six

The snow began to fall at six o'clock the next evening. Jordon sat at the conference room table and stared out the window at the fat, fluffy flakes drifting down from the heavy gray skies.

She was alone in the room. Gabriel had left almost twenty minutes ago to deal with an armed robbery that had taken place at one of the convenience stores.

She'd been distracted all day…distracted by a single kiss. It surprised her how much she'd liked that darned kiss, how much she wanted to repeat it…and more.

Neither of them had mentioned it throughout the day and she had a feeling Gabriel definitely wished it had never happened. But it had and she'd thought about it far too often as the long hours had gone by.

Releasing a deep sigh, she focused back

on the files in front of her. Although neither of them had said it out loud, they were at a dead end.

They had checked and rechecked the Rollings brothers and Billy Bond, and while they remained on the suspect list, she and Gabriel had no real evidence to point a finger at anyone. They had also dug a little deeper into the Overtons' background, but nothing in their past had raised a red flag or indicated any reason why somebody would want to hurt either one of them.

Now there was a blizzard forecast for overnight and it would probably stymie any further investigation at least through the next day or so. Jeez, she hated winter and she hated this killer.

She stared out the window once again, her thoughts flittering back to the evening before. She hadn't meant to tell Gabriel about Ralph Hicks and what had happened in that cellar. She'd thought she'd covered her anxiety well, but Gabriel had obviously picked up on her panic attack in the mirror maze.

He'd offered her just the right amount of support…a warm and strong hand holding hers and not so much sympathy that she felt guilty about sharing the events of that dark moment in her past.

He'd seen her more vulnerable, more fragile than she liked anyone to see her, but for some reason Gabriel felt safe. She knew instinctively that he was a man who would keep all of her secrets. Funny. She was a woman who didn't trust easily and yet within seven days she trusted Gabriel implicitly.

Not that any of that mattered. Once they caught the killer she'd go back to Kansas City, and within a month or two Gabriel probably wouldn't even remember her name. She wasn't sure why that thought depressed her a bit.

"Sorry about that," he said as he breezed back into the room.

"Not a problem. I know as head of this department you have lots of other things to attend to besides this case."

"Thank God I've got good men and women working with me and for the most part the department practically runs itself." He sank down in the chair across from hers and raked a hand through his thick, shiny hair. "I assigned a couple of men to investigate the armed robbery, but before I could get out of my office, I got a butt-chewing phone call from the mayor."

She raised an eyebrow. "Does he think we're not doing whatever we can to solve this?"

"He was all puffed up like a peacock and talking about his responsibility to the town. He reminded me that a serial killer running amok hurts the tourist trade Branson depends on, as if I'm too dense to know that."

"You might be a silly man, but I would never call you dense," Jordon said in an effort to lighten the dark frustration in his eyes.

It worked. His eyes lightened a bit and he leaned back in his chair. "What I'd like to be right now is a magician. I'd like to wave a magic wand and have all the answers to solve this case in my hand once and for all."

"Unfortunately, we're both short on magic wands at the moment," she replied. "Face it, partner. We've conducted a solid, thorough investigation but we're kind of at a dead end at the moment. We've hit a brick wall."

He leaned forward and released a deep sigh. "I know and it's frustrating as hell."

"Look on the bright side. The perp could attack me at any moment and then I'll nab him," she said lightly.

His gaze darkened once again. "Jordon, don't even joke about that." He scooted his chair out and stood, walked to the window and peered outside. "We probably need to head out of here. The snow is coming down pretty hard. We should also stop someplace on the way and pick you up some supplies in case I can't get to you first thing in the morning."

"Don't worry about supplies—I'll be fine. Before you arrived for breakfast this morning, Joan told me no matter how bad the weather gets, breakfast will be served as usual and she'd make sure additional meals would be available if we all get snowed in."

"Should we pick you up a sub sandwich or something else for later tonight?" His gaze once again went out the window.

"Not necessary. I'm still full from the burgers we ate earlier. I've also got some chips and peanuts left in the room if I get the munchies. I'll be fine for the rest of the night." She got up and pulled on her coat.

As they left the building to get into Gabriel's car, she was surprised to see how quickly the snow was piling up on the road. Already a couple of inches of new snow had fallen on everything.

"Just drop me off and get yourself home safe and sound. The roads look like they're already getting treacherous," she said.

Minutes later her words proved true as Gabriel slowly maneuvered the snow-covered streets with blowing snow that made visibility difficult.

She grasped the edges of her seat as the back wheels slid out and he quickly corrected. A muscle throbbed in his jawline as he frowned in concentration. They didn't speak until he reached the Diamond Cove parking lot.

"Don't wait another minute. Get someplace safe for the night," she said as she unbuckled her seat belt.

"I'll call you in the morning," he replied.

She nodded and got out of the car. The wind stole her breath and the snow stung her face and any bare skin as she hurried up the path that would take her to her room. When she reached her door she looked behind her, grateful to see the faint red glow of Gabriel's taillights as he drove away.

She hated winter more than she hated fried liver, more than she despised her ex-husband. She hoped Gabriel got home safe and sound. This was definitely not a good night to be out on the roads.

Her fingers trembled from the frigid air as she put her key into the doorknob and opened the door.

A person exploded out of the room toward her. She had only a second to register a black ski mask, a black or navy coat and the glint of the long, sharp knife as it slashed at her.

She stumbled backward, dropped her purse and fumbled for her gun as she raised her other arm defensively in front of her. She gasped as the blade sliced through the arm of her coat.

Before she could clear her gun from her holster, the figure shoved past her and ran toward the woods. Jordon nearly fell backward, but quickly regained her balance and followed. There was no way she was going to let the perp get away.

"Halt, or I'll shoot," she cried just before the person darted behind a tree.

Jordon raced ahead, the wind howling in her ears and her face and fingers freezing. She had no time to process the attack that had just occurred, a surprise attack that might have killed her. All of her training kicked in and she had only one goal in mind.

This was the perfect opportunity to bring him down. She refused to let the cold and the near-blinding conditions stop her. She absolutely refused to give in to any fear that tried to take hold of her. She didn't have time for fear.

There was no question in her mind that this was the serial killer they sought. He'd obviously hoped to stab her in the chest, to incapacitate her and then finish her off, just like he'd done to Sandy Peters.

If he'd been successful just moments before in his attack, then Gabriel or somebody else would have found her body on the porch sometime the next morning.

The only sound in the woods was the sharp pants of her own breaths as she raced forward and tried to see the dark, deadly figure who shared the area with her.

She paused and swiped at the snow on her face. Where had he gone? Was he hiding behind a tree just waiting to strike out at her again?

Was he behind her? She whirled around, every nerve tense and her heartbeat racing frantically. Her head filled with images of Samantha Kent, who had entered these woods to take pictures but instead had wound up stabbed in the back.

Swirling wind-driven snow made it impossible for her to see more than five feet in front of her. Her lungs ached with the freezing air.

Each tree she passed was a potential hiding place. Every tree in front of her could hide the knife-wielding killer. She walked slowly now, pausing often to listen to see if she could hear anything, but there was nothing but the thundering boom of her heartbeat in her head.

Bitter disappointment filled her as she realized she had no idea where he'd gone. It was possible he wasn't even in the woods anymore.

The wind cut through her, and her face and fingers had gone numb. The snow was coming down so hard now she could barely see her hand in front of her face. It was a whiteout condition.

She had to give it up. It was foolish to hunt a person in these circumstances, especially not knowing the area or if her prey was even still nearby.

She turned to head back to her room and froze in her tracks. She was in a snow globe and completely disoriented. She hadn't paid attention to the direction she'd run.

Was her cabin in front of her or to the left? Was it behind her or to the right? How far away was she from her room? How long had she been running?

Squinting, she tried to see something that would orient her, but there was nothing but snow and wind. She was in trouble. She hadn't been truly scared before, but now she was terrified. She was lost in a blizzard and had no idea where to go.

IT WAS GOING to be a long night. Jordon had assumed Gabriel was going to go home to ride out the storm in the comfort of his own home, but that wasn't happening.

As chief of police, he needed to be out on the road, seeing to stranded motorists or any accidents that were certain to occur with this kind of weather.

He'd left her and driven straight back to the station, where the garage mechanic had put snow chains on his tires. He should have had them put on earlier in the day before the storm was upon them, but he'd been busy.

Thankfully, it took only a few minutes and then he headed for the main drag, grateful to see that it appeared everyone had taken the storm warnings seriously.

Branson appeared like a ghost town. All the stores and restaurants had closed up. Shows had been canceled and there was virtually nobody on the streets.

With the near-whiteout conditions, he intended to park in one of the lots in the middle of the strip and ride out the worst of the storm. Hopefully, from here he could respond quickly to anyone who needed help. His police radio crackled as his men on duty gave updates from where they were located.

He'd just parked when his cell phone rang. A jangle of nerves coursed through him as he recognized the number as Jordon's.

"Jordon?"

"I'm sorry…I'm lost, Gabriel. I'm lost and so cold."

He sat up straighter, his heart racing. "Jordon, where are you?"

"In the woods. I'm someplace in the woods. He came after me and I chased him, but now I don't know where I am. There's so much snow. Everything is white, so white." Panic screamed from her voice and a sickness surged inside him.

"Jordon, stay where you are. I'm coming to find you."

"Okay, and, Gabriel, please hurry."

He was already racing down the street as fast as the conditions would allow him, which wasn't half-fast enough for his panicked alarm. Damn the snow that now fell in sheets.

He kept her on the phone as he radioed for more men to meet him at Diamond Cove. Once he'd called for help, she told him in a halting voice about the person waiting for her in her room and attacking her with a knife.

His heartbeat thundered inside his chest. She'd nearly been stabbed but he couldn't fully process that now. The biggest threat to her at the moment was the weather, and if she'd run from her room as soon as Gabriel had left the bed-and-breakfast, then she'd been out in the elements far too long.

By the time he reached Diamond Cove, her chattering teeth were audible over the phone as she kept up a stream of conversation.

He was grateful to see two of his men already there and waiting for him. "Agent James is someplace in the woods. We'll stick together and cover the area," he said to them. "It's also possible that our killer is someplace out here, so stay alert.

"Jordon, we're here and we have flashlights," he said into his cell phone. "Let me know when you see or hear us."

"I'm officially now a snow cone. A cherry snow cone because that's my favorite flavor. If I was from Italy I'd be an Italian ice," she said and released a small burst of laughter that bordered on hysteria.

He wasn't surprised that she'd defaulted to humor. He'd known her long enough to realize it was her way to deal with stress or fear. "We're on our way, Jordon."

"Maybe it's better to be a snow angel than a snow cone," she said and rambled on about making snow angels when she'd been younger and had lived in Denver with her parents.

Gabriel led the men to her suite, where the door was still open, her key remained in the doorknob and her purse was on the ground. He threw her purse inside the room, pulled the key out, shoved it into his pocket and then closed the door.

It was impossible to follow any footprints. The wind and the falling snow had already covered whatever prints there might have been. As they stepped off the porch and entered the woods, all three of them began to yell her name as their flashlights scanned the snowy landscape.

Gabriel could only pray they were going in the right direction. After only a few steps, the cold ached inside him and his face stung. He couldn't imagine how frozen she must be.

It was slow going as visibility was nearly down to nothing, and the men walked side by side so that none of them would get lost, as well.

As Jim and Bill yelled her name, Gabriel kept the phone pressed tightly against his ear. "Maybe I'm a snow woman," Jordon said. "If somebody is making me into a snow woman then I definitely want bigger boobs."

Gabriel was grateful he didn't have her on speaker. He knew without a doubt she wouldn't want anyone else hearing this conversation but him.

How much longer could she stay out here in

the cold? She already sounded half-delirious. He was also aware that she could be vulnerable to another attack by whoever had gone after her in the first place.

His brain flashed with visions of what Samantha Kent must have looked like when Billy Bond had found her. According to the groundskeeper, she'd been facedown on the ground and bleeding out from the vicious stab wounds she'd suffered.

They had to find Jordon. They had to find her right now. The wind seemed to swallow the men's cries and Gabriel realized Jordon had stopped babbling.

"Jordon?" he asked urgently.

"I'm here...I think I heard somebody shouting my name."

"Scream...scream as loud as you can," he replied. He took the phone away from his ear.

A raw, ear-piercing scream shattered the silence. It not only sounded from the cell phone in his hand, but also from someplace to the left of them.

"This way," Jim said urgently and headed in that direction.

Suddenly she was in front of them. Snow covered her dark hair and her shoulders, and her eyes glowed wild in the light. "Jordon!"

Gabriel shut off the cell phone and stuffed it into his pocket as he ran toward her.

"Gabriel!" She met him and slammed her body into his, her arms wrapping tightly around his waist. "Thank God you found me," she said with a half sob.

He held her tight for only a couple of seconds. "Let's get you out of here." With his arm around her shoulders, the four of them headed back to the cabin.

First he wanted her safe and warm, and then he wanted to know every single detail that had led up to her being out in the woods in a blizzard.

Once they reached her suite, he thanked Bill and Jim and they left to get back on the road to help anyone else who might be in trouble.

Gabriel's first order of business was Jordon. As she stood shivering, he shrugged out of his coat and then pulled hers off. "Sit," he said and pointed to the chair next to the fireplace. He turned on the flames and then hurried to the bathroom for a towel.

His blood ran cold as he saw that the window in the small room was open and the screen was nowhere to be seen. He grabbed a hand towel and used it to slam it shut. He tried to lock it, but the lock didn't work. This answered how the perp had gotten inside.

He took a couple of bath towels from the stack on the back of the commode and hurried back to her. She'd taken off her boots and socks and rubbed her bare feet together. At least she didn't appear to be drowsy or suffering from hypothermia.

"I'm sorry. I didn't mean to be any trouble." Her voice broke with a hiccuping sob.

"Here, dry off your hair," he replied softly. She did as he instructed, and he went to the small closet and pulled down a blanket that was folded on the top shelf.

He wrapped the blanket around her. "Let me see your fingers."

He took one of her hands in his, grateful to see her fingertips were red but didn't show any indication of frostbite. "Now your feet."

She hesitated a moment but then raised her legs so he could grab her ankles. Her toenails were painted a pearly pink and he was grateful again that her toes were cold, but didn't appear to suffer frostbite.

"Okay," he said and she lowered her feet back to the floor. For the first time since he'd answered her call on his phone, his stomach slowly began to unclench. He leaned over her, pulled the blanket more tightly around her and then sat opposite her chair on the edge of the bed.

The beige blanket emphasized the bright green of her eyes and her dark, damp tousled hair. She looked so fragile and he wanted nothing more than to pull her into his arms and comfort her…warm her. But he had business to attend to.

"Feeling better?"

"A little," she replied.

"Now, tell me exactly what happened after I dropped you off here," he said.

She grimaced and sat up straighter in the chair. "He was waiting for me in here. I opened the door and was met by a knife. He tried to stab me but thankfully only sliced through the arm of my coat. Before I could grab my gun, he pushed past me and ran into the woods. I didn't want him to get away."

Her eyes blazed bright. "I didn't think about the weather. I didn't think of anything except catching him. But it didn't take long for the storm to make it impossible for me to find him."

"Did you get a good look at him?" He asked the question even knowing that if she'd been able to identify him she would have already done so.

"Black ski mask, black or navy coat." She frowned. "It all happened so fast."

"Height...weight?" he asked.

"I...I'm not sure. Maybe taller than me? And with his coat it was difficult to tell body weight." She shrugged the blanket off her shoulders and expelled a deep breath of obvious frustration. "I'm an FBI agent and I can't even tell you exactly what my attacker looked like. I can't even tell you what material his coat was made of."

"Jordon, cut yourself some slack. You were caught by surprise in the middle of a snowstorm. Whoever it was, entry was made through the bathroom window. It looks like the lock doesn't connect right."

She frowned and pulled the blanket back around her shoulders. "I wonder who around here knew the lock wasn't working properly?"

"Our handyman, Ed Rollings, might know," he said grimly.

She stared at him for a long moment. "Don't tell me again you want me to move to another motel. You're right—I was caught by surprise tonight, but that won't happen again and I'm not going anywhere."

Gabriel grimaced. It was as if she'd read his mind and he wanted to shake her for her stubbornness. He walked over to the window and moved the curtain aside to peer outside.

There appeared to be about five inches of snow already on the ground and it was still coming down fast and furiously. Even if there hadn't been any weather conditions to contend with, his decision would be the same.

He turned back to look at her. "I'm not leaving you alone here until that window is fixed, and that won't happen before tomorrow."

"So, I get a snuggle buddy for the night. I like it." Her lips curved into a smile and her eyes held an inviting light that twisted Gabriel's gut with a new kind of tension.

Chapter Seven

She couldn't get warm.

She felt as if she'd never be truly warm again. Even with the blanket clutched tightly around her shoulders and the knowledge that Gabriel was going to be with her through the night, Jordon still possessed a stubborn inner chill that wouldn't go away.

It wasn't the fear of the close call with the killer that kept her frozen, but rather the moments when she'd been surrounded by the harshness of winter. At least that was what she told herself.

Gabriel wandered the room, obviously looking for something…anything the killer might have left behind before his attack. His shoulders were rigid with tension and his frown was as deep, as dark as she'd ever seen it.

How she wished things had played out differently tonight. If not for the damned winter weather she was certain she would have managed to capture the killer and the case would have been solved.

It would be nice if they found the killer's body in the woods sometime tomorrow, frozen to death and no longer a threat to anyone. But she knew fate wouldn't be so kind.

They wouldn't find anything in the woods. The snowstorm would have effectively erased or covered any evidence the killer might have left behind.

Gabriel disappeared into the bathroom, and she closed her eyes and tried to access any minute detail about the attacker that she might not have thought of before. Hidden face, dark bulky coat and big, wicked knife—that was all she'd seen and it wasn't enough.

She'd been anticipating a potential attack, had been so careful, so cautious whenever she'd come and gone from her room. In her wildest nightmares she'd never dreamed the danger would explode out at her from inside her suite.

The whole room felt slightly tainted now. Her privacy, her safe place had been violated by the mere presence of the killer. Still, she was more determined than ever to remain here.

"I should go get a print kit from my car and

see if I can lift anything," Gabriel said as he came back out of the bathroom.

"It wouldn't do any good. He had on gloves." She'd seen the knife and she now realized she'd also seen the hand that held it. "Big, black gloves. You won't find anything in here. You didn't find anything in Sandy Peters's room or at the other two crime scenes. This creep is careful and he still hasn't made a mistake."

Once again he sat on the edge of the bed facing her. She pulled the blanket closer around her throat. "I don't think it was Ed."

He sat up straighter. "Why do you say that?"

She frowned and once again went over every detail of the surprise assault. "Ed is a bit heavyset and I think our killer is leaner."

"Even if it wasn't Ed that still leaves Glen, Kevin and Billy Bond as potential suspects. None of them are particularly big men."

"Billy Bond would know the woods intimately. As groundskeeper, he probably knows the trails better than anyone else," she replied. "The person I was chasing didn't seem to be running willy-nilly. He seemed to know exactly where he was going."

"You shouldn't have gone out there all alone. You could have been killed, Jordon."

His gaze remained dark and troubled as he looked at her.

"Then I would have died doing what I love. Besides, it worked out okay. The only way things would have been better is if I'd managed to get him and you hadn't had to ride to my rescue. Did you search all of the woods after Samantha Kent was killed?"

"Every inch of them," he replied.

"Is there anything on the property besides trees and brush?"

"A couple of old outbuildings," he said. "One of them is nothing more than a lean-to shed where lawn equipment is stored. The other one is just a little bit more substantial."

"Substantial enough to harbor somebody overnight in a snowstorm?"

He ran a hand down his jaw where a five o'clock shadow had begun to appear. "Doubtful. There are no windows or doors in it and it lists badly to one side."

She couldn't control a shiver that overtook her as she remembered the horror of the frigid temperature and the snow that had been everywhere.

"You're still cold. I saw a little coffeepot on the vanity in the bathroom. Do you want me to make some?"

"Not unless you want a cup." She knew

what would warm her up. He could. If he'd just wrap her in his arms and kiss her, the inner chill would finally ease. If he took her to bed and made love to her, she'd be wonderfully warm.

With the deep frown cutting across his forehead and the set of his shoulders, the last thing he appeared to have on his mind was any kind of intimacy with her. He probably thought he was going to spend the night on one of the chairs rather than sharing the bed with her.

But he had kissed her and his lips had held the heat of desire and the taste of deep yearning. In the past week she'd felt his attraction toward her. Furtive heated glances, a casual touch that lingered a little too long. Whether he knew it or not, he'd definitely been sending signals she'd received.

"There's only one way for me to get warm," she said. She shrugged off the blanket and stood. "I need a nice hot bubble bath."

His eyes widened. "Now?"

"Right this very minute." She walked over to the oversize tub and started the water. He turned on the bed to continue to stare at her.

She ignored him and adjusted the water temperature and then added some of the lilac-scented bubble bath to the tub. When she looked at him again, his eyes were still widened with an expression she couldn't quite read.

He cleared his throat. "If you're going to take a bath then I'll just go sit in the bathroom until you're finished," he said.

"Don't be silly. If it makes you that uncomfortable then you can just sit there and stare at the fire." She began to unbutton her blouse.

He whipped his head around to face the opposite direction but not before she saw the searing desire, the raw, stark hunger that lit his eyes momentarily.

"You like baths," he said, his voice sounding slightly strained.

"I love a nice soak. Now that I think about it, I guess it's one of my major stress relievers," she replied.

By the time she'd stripped off the rest of her clothes, the tub was full of steamy, scented water. She eased down into the warm depths and pushed the button to get the jets working.

Leaning back in the tub built for two, she knew it wouldn't be enough. She wanted a bath, but at the moment what she needed, what she wished for more than anything was the man who sat on the bed.

She wouldn't be happy, she wouldn't find the warmth she craved until Gabriel held her in his arms.

TORTURE.

The sounds of sloshing water, the whir of the jets, and the faint sensual moans she emitted were sheer torture to Gabriel.

He stared intently into the fireplace, but instead of seeing the dancing flames there, his head filled with visions of a very bare Jordon in the tub.

Her skin would be warm and soft and sweetly scented by the fragrance of lilacs. He was jealous of the jetted water that swirled around her naked body. He was on fire with the desire for her that had simmered inside him for the last week.

The memory of the kiss they had shared burned in his head. Her lips had been so soft, so hot, and just thinking about it heated his blood.

"I think this is a perfect night to open this bottle of complimentary wine," she said. "Would you like a glass?" There was a sweet invitation in her voice.

She was seducing him.

It was evident in her tone of voice, in the fact that she'd gotten into the tub with him sitting right here. She was seducing him and he was helplessly faltering in his desire to not respond.

Don't turn around, a little voice whispered

in his head. He somehow knew that if he turned around, if he saw her in that tub, he'd be lost.

Still, even knowing that he was making a mistake, in spite of all the internal alarms that rang in his head, he stood and turned around.

Her beauty squeezed the air out of his lungs and shot a burst of fiery adrenaline through his veins. Her hair looked even more charmingly curly than it had before, and her creamy shoulders and a hint of her breasts were visible above the bubbles.

He had no conscious memory of crossing the room, but suddenly he stood by the edge of the tub. She smiled up at him and held out a glass of wine. "Why don't you join me. The water's just fine."

She was a wicked temptation, and any good sense he had fled beneath the sensual assault she presented to him. He was cold, and the only way he could get warm was to join her in the tub.

Her eyes beckoned him like a silent siren song. As if in a trance, he took off his belt and dropped it to the floor and then unbuttoned his shirt and shrugged it off. He was making a mistake and someplace in the back of his mind he knew it, but nothing short of the apocalypse could keep him out of that tub.

He took out his gun and set it on the tiled area next to the bathtub and then kicked off his shoes, bent down and peeled off his socks. As he unfastened his slacks and stepped out of them, that inner voice whispered that this was his last chance to stop the madness, but he didn't listen.

He'd never been a shy man. He knew he was physically fit, but as he took off his boxers and then eased down into the tub, the smile Jordon gave him made him feel like Adonis himself.

She was curled up on one side of the tub and he was on the other. His legs stretched out to the left. She did the same so they didn't touch each other. She leaned forward and handed him the glass of wine and then grabbed hers.

"Here's to warm baths and snuggle buddies," she toasted and then clinked her glass with his.

He didn't draw a full, deep breath until she leaned back again. If he didn't touch her then there would be no harm, no foul.

If this was the only intimacy they shared, then they could face each other in the morning without any regrets. He took a big swallow of the wine.

"I'll admit, this does have its merits," he said as the warm water swirled around him.

She smiled. "And you're going to smell like a beautiful spring flower when you get out." She downed her wine and then poured herself some more. She held the bottle out to splash more in his glass but he shook his head.

"I'm good." The last thing he needed was to add too much alcohol to the fire. Besides, he was already half intoxicated by her.

She took another sip from her glass and then set it on the side of the tub, closed her eyes and released a sigh of obvious pleasure.

How could she look so relaxed? Only hours before, she had been attacked by a killer and faced freezing to death in the middle of a snowstorm.

He'd wanted to be angry with her for chasing the perp without calling for backup, without giving any thought to the consequences. However, it was difficult to be angry with her when he knew he would have reacted the same way.

It was equally difficult to sit across from her and gaze at her without wanting her. The bubbles were slowly dissipating and in desperation he looked up at the ceiling. The last thing he needed was to do something stupid that might complicate their partnership.

The water sloshed and he knew she was changing positions, but he kept his gaze upward. "Gabriel? Would you mind washing my back?"

Every muscle in his body tensed as he looked at her once again. She held out a wet washcloth and a small beige soap bar, and there was not only a warm invitation in her eyes but also that damned soft seduction. "Please?"

He was helpless to deny her. Hell, he was helpless to deny himself. He took the washcloth and soap from her and moved his legs so that he was sitting cross-legged, and she sat the same way directly in front of him with her back turned toward him.

He wasn't touching her—the washcloth was, he told himself as he caressed the soapy cloth over her slender back. But he knew he was only fooling himself. He wanted her and it was obvious she wanted him, too.

Good sense be damned, he knew with a sweet inevitability there was no way they would exit this room in the morning without having made love if that was what she wanted.

As soon as the thought filled his head, she turned to face him. The washcloth and soap slid from his hand the second she leaned into him.

Her bare breasts pressed against his chest at the same time their lips met. As the kiss deepened, he stretched out his legs and pulled her fully on top of him.

Warm soft skin, hot lips and the heady scent of lilacs cast all other thoughts out of his head. There was just him and Jordon and this single night.

"I want you, Gabriel," she said softly as their kiss ended. Her eyes shone with a brilliance he could drown in.

"I want you, too, Jordon." The words issued forth from the very depths of him.

She placed a finger over his lips. "I love the way my name sounds on your lips. I love the way your body feels against mine. Now I think it's time we move this to the bed." She moved away from him and hit the knob that would empty the water.

He stepped out of the tub and onto the bath mat and then grabbed one of the fluffy over-size towels and quickly dried himself off. He took a second towel and beckoned her out of the tub.

He'd officially lost his mind and he knew it, but they were both in too deep to stop now. She stood with her back to him and he began drying her shoulders. As he did so he leaned forward to kiss just behind one of her earlobes.

She leaned her head back and released a small moan that shot fire through his blood. He moved the towel down the length of her slender back, over her perfectly rounded butt and then down her shapely legs.

The tight control he'd maintained since the moment she'd started the water in the tub snapped. He dropped the towel, scooped her up in his arms and carried her to the bed.

There was no time to fold down blankets or turn out the lights. They were on each other like two hungry animals. He took her mouth in another kiss and reveled in the full-body contact with her.

This time when he broke the kiss, he moved his mouth slowly down the length of her neck, across her delicate collarbone and then to the raised nipple of one of her breasts. He teased it with his tongue, loving the taste of her and the way her fingers splayed in his hair as if she couldn't get enough of him.

He definitely couldn't get enough of her. He raised his head and gazed at her. "You are so beautiful, so perfect."

"I almost believe it when you say it," she replied in a husky voice.

With his desire a barely controlled beast inside him, he continued to explore her body. It was only when his fingers touched the raised scars on her left hip that desire was tempered by empathy and an anger that she had ever been in a cellar where a madman had played on her body with a lit cigarette.

He ran his fingers over the raised area and then followed the caress with his lips. He'd like to be able to kiss away not only the physical scar, but also the memory of that time, of that horrible pain she had to have endured. He wished he could kiss away the fear that she must have experienced knowing she was in the hands of a brutal serial killer.

He moved his hand to her inner thigh and then to the soft folds of her center. She moaned and whispered his name as he moved his fingers faster against her.

She arched her hips upward to meet him, and within minutes she gasped and stiffened as she climaxed. She shuddered and reached up to grab his shoulders.

Her eyes glowed a deep green. "Take me now, Gabriel. I want you inside of me."

He didn't hesitate. He moved between her thighs and slowly entered her. Her warm, moist heat surrounded him as her fingernails dug into his back.

He fought to maintain control, to last for as long as he possibly could. But as he began to stroke inside her, intense pleasure washed over him and he feared he'd lose it far too quickly.

His lips took hers once again in a fiery kiss that stole all thought from his mind. She met him thrust for thrust as fevered pants escaped them both.

She cried out his name as she stiffened against him and then moaned as she found her release once again. Gabriel's climax came hard and fast. He groaned and half collapsed on top of her.

He remained there only a moment and then rolled to the side of her and waited for his heartbeat to resume a more normal pace.

She rose up on one elbow and gazed at him with a soft smile. "I don't know about you, but I think that was pretty amazing."

He reached up and caressed her cheek. "'Amazing' doesn't even begin to describe it."

She leaned over and kissed him, a soft sweet kiss that stirred him on a completely different level altogether. "And now I'm wonderfully exhausted. All I need to do is get you out of this bed so that we can get under the covers."

She got off the bed and he did the same.

As she stood, he saw the heart-shaped scar on her hip and once again his heart squeezed tight for the fear, the pain she must have gone through.

"Get your gun," he said. "I'll be right back." He took his gun from the edge of the bathtub and then went into the bathroom and closed the door behind him.

This night had been all kinds of wrong. He checked the window to make sure it was properly locked and then stepped up to the mirror and stared at his reflection.

From the moment the attacker had leaped out at Jordon, mistakes had been made, first by her and then by him. Making love to her had definitely been a huge mistake. Hell, they hadn't even used protection.

She touched him like no other woman had ever done before in his life. She made him laugh and she made him think. He wanted to know all of her thoughts, every one of her innermost emotions and dreams.

She was exactly the kind of woman he wanted in his life and she couldn't be more wrong for him. She'd told him she wasn't interested in marriage. Footloose and fancy-free—that was the way she wanted to live her life. They just wanted different things in their lives.

Starting tomorrow, he had to distance himself from her. They had to get back on the course of being strictly partners trying to hunt down a killer and nothing more.

But first, he was going to return to the bedroom and climb into bed with her. She would snuggle against him and he would want her all over again.

He leaned closer to his reflection. "Bonehead," he whispered to the man in the mirror.

Chapter Eight

Jordon awoke before dawn. Gabriel was spooned around her back with his arm thrown across her waist and his deep, even breathing warmed the back of her neck.

She closed her eyes again and embraced the moment of feeling loved even though she knew it was a false sentiment. Gabriel Walters could never love a woman like her. Nobody could really love her. Still, it was nice to pretend for a little while.

Certainly making love with him had rocked her world. He'd been so passionate and so wonderfully intense. He'd made her feel incredibly beautiful and desired.

They'd come together again sometime in the middle of the night, and then their lovemaking had been sleepy and slow and all kinds of wonderful.

However, she knew when dawn broke and a

new day began, it would be business as usual between them. She didn't expect the soft glow in her heart to remain. She wasn't here for romance. She didn't *do* romance. She was here to catch a killer.

She remained in bed, wrapped in Gabriel's warmth and listening to her heartbeat mirror the slow steady beat of his until the sound of a snowblower shattered the silence. Gabriel stirred and slowly unwound himself from her.

"Good morning," he said as he sat up and raked a hand through his hair.

"Back at you," she replied.

He leaned over and grabbed his cell phone from the nightstand. "Jeez, it's just after seven. I haven't slept this late since before the first murder."

She slid out of bed. "I get the bathroom first." She grabbed a fresh pair of slacks, a blouse and her underwear and then went into the bathroom.

She hoped he didn't want to talk about last night. She didn't want to hear the regrets he was probably feeling in the light of day.

While she suffered not a single regret about what they had shared, she also wasn't eager to delve too deeply into exactly what her own feelings were.

Dressing as quickly as possible, she tried

to get her head back into the game of murder and away from the night of passion. The killer was escalating in his quest. He'd almost gotten to her last night. She'd been lucky that the first knife strike hadn't hit her chest and incapacitated her.

When she left the bathroom Gabriel had already dressed and made the bed. He stood at the window with the curtain pulled back allowing a faint stream of sunshine to seep into the room.

"If you don't like the weather in Missouri just wait a minute and it changes," she said.

He turned away from the window with a nod. "It's hard to believe we were in blizzard conditions last night. It looks like the sun is going to shine today."

She walked over to stand next to him and peered outside. The morning sun sparkled on the five or six inches of additional snow that had fallen overnight. In the distance she saw Billy Bond working a snowblower around the dining room porch and Ted Overton was shoveling off the paths in front of the cabins.

"It looks like everyone is working hard except us," she said.

"Why don't we head in for coffee and breakfast and then we'll get to work."

Within minutes they were both in their

coats and snow boots and heading toward the dining room. Billy and his snowblower had disappeared, but Ted greeted them on the path with a quick, cheerful "good morning" as he continued to shovel.

WHEN THEY ENTERED the dining room, not only was Joan there, but also Jason and Hannah were seated at the table eating breakfast. Billy had apparently come in to get warm and stood by the fireplace sipping a cup of coffee.

"Good morning, everyone," Gabriel said.

They all returned his greeting except Billy, who gave a curt nod and then turned to face the fire. All of Jordon's muscles tensed. Was it guilt that had him facing away from them or just the desire to warm up?

They each got a cup of coffee and then sat at the table with the two teenagers while Joan scurried into the kitchen to see to their breakfast.

"Billy, why don't you join us?" Gabriel said. His tone of voice indicated it was a command, not a simple request. Billy got the message, for he moved away from the fire and sat in the chair opposite Jordon.

She stared at him but he refused to meet her gaze. He looked at a place just over her shoulder and then into his cup as if the contents were of great interest.

Was he the person who had been in her room last night? Was he the cold-blooded killer they sought? He'd probably know about the window lock and could have even set it so that it appeared to be secure when it wasn't.

"Heck of a night," Gabriel said. He took a sip of his coffee then turned to look at the groundskeeper. "How are the roads out there?"

"Side streets are a mess, but it looked like the road crews had already hit the main streets when I came in," he replied.

"Where did you ride out the storm, Billy?"

The man shot Gabriel a quick glance. "At home, where any sane person would be in that kind of weather," he replied.

"Anyone with you?" Jordon asked.

For the first time since they'd entered the room, his gaze met hers. Cold and flat, his eyes stared into hers and she fought against an inner chill. "It wasn't exactly a good night for socializing."

"What about for a walk in the woods?" Gabriel asked. Jason and Hannah had stopped any pretense at eating as they listened intently to the conversation.

"I don't know what you're talking about."

Billy took a sip from his cup and then leaned back in the chair. "Why would I go for a walk in the woods in the middle of a snowstorm?"

"That's what we're trying to figure out. Jordon thought she saw somebody in the woods last night," Gabriel said. It was apparent by the way he framed his words that he intended to play the attack close to his chest.

"Well, it wasn't me," Billy said. "Getting out in weather like that for a walk would be just plain stupid. I might be many things, but I'm not that dumb."

At that moment Ted came in from outside. "Billy, you warmed up enough to get back to work?"

"I am." Billy got up from the table, put on his coat and then headed out the door.

"Do you think Billy is the killer?" Hannah asked half-breathlessly.

"We're still investigating," Jordon replied as the snowblower outside once again started up.

"He's always been kind of weird," Jason said and then popped a piece of bacon into his mouth.

Ted wore a deep frown. "Is Billy a suspect?"

"Like Agent James said, we're still investigating," Gabriel replied.

Joan entered the room carrying their plates

and then sat at the table next to her husband. "I see you two got through last night okay. According to the weatherman, we're supposed to get above-freezing temperatures tomorrow and it's supposed to be in the mid-forties for the rest of the week."

"Ah, sweet music to my ears," Jordon said. She took a sip of her coffee and then looked at Ted. "I was wondering about the outbuildings in the woods. Gabriel said there is a lean-to shed out there and also a building that's a little more substantial."

"That's right," Ted replied. "They're really nothing but eyesores. One of my goals for this spring is to tear them both down and put up a nice, new shed."

"Is there electricity out there?" Jordon asked.

"Not in the lean-to shed but in the other building there is, although we don't use that building at all," Ted replied.

"Mom, can we be excused?" Jason asked Joan.

"Go ahead, but get your morning chores done. Just because you have a snow day at school doesn't mean you don't keep your usual routine."

"We know, we know," Hannah replied, earning her a stern look from Joan. The two kids quickly got up, grabbed their coats and left.

"What's with all the questions about the outbuildings?" Ted asked.

"Jordon was attacked last night and whoever did it ran into the woods," Gabriel replied.

"Attacked?" Joan raised a hand to her lips in horror. "What happened?"

"He was waiting for me in the room. He got in through the bathroom window. He tried to stab me and then ran off into the woods," Jordon explained.

"Oh, sweet Lord," Joan exclaimed. "I'm so glad you're okay."

"I'm fine," Jordon assured her. "The arm of my coat was the only casualty."

"Thank goodness," Joan replied, her voice still filled with a touch of shock.

"That lock on the window in Jordon's room needs to be replaced or fixed," Gabriel said. "And hopefully it can be done today."

"Ed should be in within the next couple of hours. I'll get him right on it," Ted replied and then looked at Jordon. "Did you see who it was?" He grimaced. "I guess you didn't since you're sitting here instead of making an arrest."

Jordon shook her head. "He had on a ski

mask and it was impossible for me to make an identification."

"We're hoping maybe there might be something in the woods or in one of those outbuildings that might yield a clue," Gabriel said.

"I certainly hope so. I want this nightmare to be over," Joan replied fervently.

Jordon ate quickly as did Gabriel. If they were going to head into the woods to see what they could find, then she wanted to do it sooner rather than later.

The very idea of traipsing through the snow made her want to shiver, but if they found something that would help them catch the murderer then it would be worth every agonizingly cold moment.

It was almost eight thirty by the time they left the dining room. There was no sign of Billy and the sound of the snowblower had stopped.

"You might want to put your gun in your coat pocket so you can zip up your coat," Gabriel said and his breaths hung on frosty puffs.

"I definitely want my coat zipped," she replied. "That hot beach in Florida would be nice right about now."

"A beach anywhere sounds good to me," Gabriel agreed.

They took off walking toward the woods. Both of them had their guns in hand.

"I've got to confess, I'm not feeling optimistic about us finding anything out here," she said.

Gabriel smiled at her, that beautiful smile that sparked warmth through her entire body. "I thought you were the optimist in this partnership." His smile faded and he stopped in his tracks, his eyes slightly darker in hue. "Do we need to talk about last night?"

"As far as I'm concerned, there's nothing to talk about. We were just two cold souls who warmed each other up on a cold wintry night." She forced a lightness into her voice. As crazy as it sounded, it had been more than just a hot hookup for her.

He held her gaze for a long moment, his features radiating with an emotion she couldn't discern. "Okay, then let's get this done." He trudged ahead and she quickly followed.

As they got deeper into the woods, Jordon tried not to remember the panic that had nearly crippled her the night before when she'd been lost in a snow globe.

She also had to swallow down the fear that had gripped her, knowing that at any moment a knife could stab her and she would become the fourth victim to die at Diamond Cove.

There were places where the snow had drifted and others that appeared barely touched by the new snowfall. The tree branches sparkled in the sunlight. It would have been a beautiful winter wonderland if they weren't hunting for clues that would lead them to a savage killer.

They walked slowly, scanning the area silently and with focused concentration. If only they could find a scrap of material from a torn coat, something dropped out of a pocket, anything that would identify who had been in her room and had tried to stab her.

When they approached the lean-to shack that Gabriel had described, he motioned for her to go to the left and he went to the right.

She tightened her grip on her gun, even though she didn't really expect trouble. Whoever had been in the woods last night would have beat feet to get out of the area long before now.

The shed held a riding lawn mower, rakes and shovels, and other yard equipment, but nothing that didn't belong there. They checked the entire structure but didn't find anything that would indicate that anyone had been there the night before.

The sun grew warmer on her shoulders as they left the shed and continued on. Once again she scanned the pristine landscape for anything that was out of place, something that didn't belong.

In the distance was the other outbuilding Gabriel had mentioned. It was bigger than the other shed and had a doorway without a door and two windows with no glass.

It appeared completely abandoned and like a stiff wind would bring it down. She couldn't imagine anyone huddling inside for the duration of the snowstorm. A sigh escaped her. This whole search had been nothing but more dead ends.

How she wished she would have been able to catch the person the night before. She'd been so taken by surprise. Somehow, she should have managed to take down the perp before he ever shoved past her and jumped off her porch.

The crack of gunfire split the air and a bullet dug into the snow at Jordon's feet. She scarcely had time to register it when Gabriel slammed his body into hers and took her down to the ground.

GABRIEL'S HEART THUNDERED as he returned fire into the building. Jordon wiggled out from beneath him. "See if you can get around to the back," she said. "I'll cover you and get behind a tree trunk."

Although his first instinct was to protect her, he reminded himself she was a trained professional and as it was they were both sitting ducks with their dark coats against the white snow. They needed cover.

He gave a curt nod. She fired into the building and he raced to the right, praying that she would manage to get behind something before a bullet found her.

As he darted to the back of a tree, he looked back and sighed in relief when he saw that she had rolled sideways and now crouched behind the trunk of a large oak.

Several more shots came from the shed, one of the bullets pinging off the tree behind which he hid. Who was in the shed? There had been nothing to indicate in the past that the killer they sought had a gun.

Jordon returned fire and Gabriel darted to another tree, moving him closer to the back of the shed. There was no way he intended to allow whoever was inside to escape.

If it was the killer, Gabriel had no idea why he would be here now. But certainly with the attack and the flight last night, he had to believe that the person they had sought was the same person shooting at them.

Adrenaline pumped through him as he moved again. Jordon was no longer in his sight, and as gunfire sounded from the shed once again, he could only hope that no bullet found her.

At least he didn't hear a scream of agony or any cry for help. But would she shout for aid if she'd been shot, or would she lie in the snow and die silently? She was so tough and obviously a lone wolf.

He made it to the rear of the shed just in time to see a figure dart out of the back door opening. He recognized the cut of the dark coat and the baggy jeans beneath. He'd seen them earlier in the dining room.

Billy Bond.

"Jordon, in the back," he yelled and took off running after Billy.

Billy ran fast, but Gabriel ran faster, fueled by anger and determination. "Billy, halt! Don't make me shoot you in the back."

Instead of shooting at him, Gabriel got close enough to lunge at his back. Billy hit the ground hard with Gabriel on top of him.

Jordon appeared and leaned down to place the barrel of her gun against the side of Billy's head. "If you twitch, I'll shoot," she said firmly.

"Please, don't shoot me!" Billy exclaimed.

"Billy, what in the hell are you doing?" Gabriel said as he got to his feet and yanked the man up by the back of his coat. As Gabriel handcuffed Billy, Jordon searched his pockets and pulled out his gun, then did a more thorough pat-down.

"It's a meth lab," Jordon said. "I ran through the shed and there's enough material in there to keep the whole state high for a very long time."

"I don't know what you're talking about," Billy replied, a surly snarl curving his lips.

"Then why were you shooting at us?" Gabriel asked as he led the man back the way they had come.

"I wasn't shooting at you. It must have been somebody else. I was just out here trimming some tree branches."

"And I'm the freaking queen of Scotland," Jordon retorted with a laugh.

Gabriel led Billy into the shed, where he looked around in stunned surprise. A hot plate was plugged into an electrical socket that hung from the lightbulb in the ceiling. Mason jars gleamed red and purple, and jugs of drain cleaner, paint thinner and a variety of other items used to make the deadly drug littered what was left of the workbench.

Anger once again ripped through Gabriel. Fighting the making and use of meth was a full-time job. It was a scourge that not only ripped apart families, but killed. And this had been going on right under his nose.

Was Billy just a dope manufacturer and dealer or was he a killer, as well?

"Let's go," he said and roughly yanked Billy out of the door.

Within minutes they were in his car and headed to the police station. They rode in silence. Gabriel drove slowly although he was eager to get Billy into an interrogation room and have a long talk. He needed to find out if they now had the killer under arrest.

Thankfully, the main roads had been cleared, but the side streets remained a grim testimony to the storm that had roared through overnight.

He felt the tension that wafted from Jordon and knew that she had the same questions that he had about Billy Bond and his potential relationship to the murders that had taken place.

Had he been the person who had attacked Jordon? Had he climbed through the window with the intention of killing her? Gabriel gripped the steering wheel tightly and tried to quell his anger.

Once at the station, he put Billy into the small interview room and then instructed his right-hand man, Lieutenant Mark Johnson, to gather up the team trained for cleaning up drug labs in the area and get out to Diamond Cove.

Jordon stood just outside the interrogation room door, peering in through the small window to where Billy sat at the table with his head in his hands.

"We now know why we thought he was a creep," she said. "He definitely had something to hide."

"A damn meth lab." Gabriel shook his head.

"And potentially our killer?" Jordon looked at him with darkened eyes.

"Let's get in there and see just how much he has to hide," Gabriel replied, hoping that this would be the end of the search for their murderer.

Billy looked up as the two of them entered the room. His smirk was gone, replaced by eyes that held nothing but despair and hopelessness.

Gabriel sat across from him and Jordon remained standing just behind Gabriel's chair. He read Billy his rights and thankfully the groundskeeper waived his right for a lawyer.

"I'm in big trouble, aren't I?" he asked.

"You're looking at fifteen years just for the drug charges. If I add in attempted murder then you're probably looking at life," Gabriel replied.

Billy's eyes widened slightly. "I wasn't trying to kill you. I just wanted to scare you off. Dumb, huh."

"Duh, we're the law. We run toward bullets, not away from them," Jordon said drily.

"Methamphetamines? What on earth were you thinking, Billy? Just how long has this been going on?"

Billy grimaced and shook his head. "My sister was diagnosed with breast cancer three months ago. She needs money for treatment and I was desperate."

"Desperate enough to murder three innocent people?" Jordon asked.

Billy's gaze shot to her and then back to Gabriel, his eyes widened once again. "Don't try to pin that on me. I don't know anything about those murders—you've got to believe me." He leaned forward, his eyes filled with fire as he held Gabriel's gaze. "I'll admit I'm guilty of the meth lab, but I did not kill those people."

A weight dropped inside Gabriel's chest and lay heavy in the pit of his stomach. He believed Billy. And if Billy wasn't their killer, then who was?

Chapter Nine

They interviewed Billy for almost two hours, and it was only when Gabriel wanted the names of anyone else involved in the meth operation that Billy finally demanded a lawyer.

He was taken to a jail cell to await a meeting with legal counsel, and Jordon and Gabriel got in his car to head back to Diamond Cove.

"I hate to admit it, but I believe him," Jordon said as she adjusted the car heater vents for maximum warmth on her face. "I believe that he wasn't in the woods last night and I believe him when he said he wasn't the person who attacked me. I just don't think Billy is our man."

"I agree and that's good news and bad news," Gabriel replied. "The good news is we can take him off our suspect list. The bad news is that means our murderer is still out here somewhere."

Jordon stared out the passenger window, her mind working over the few suspects they had left. The Rollings brothers, they were it. Was one of them the killer or was the person they sought completely off the grid, flying under their radar? That was definitely a depressing thought.

She gazed back at Gabriel. "I'm assuming we'll be checking some alibis for last night at some point today?"

"Definitely, although the first order of business is seeing to it that the window in your room is fixed."

He pulled into the Diamond Cove entrance, where two police cars and an evidence van were already parked. Several officers stood around, and it appeared that the van had been packed with all the items that had been in the shed.

"Chief," Mark greeted them as they got out of the car. "We're loaded up and ready to leave. Thank God it looked like he hadn't cooked for a couple of days and the fumes weren't too bad at all. It definitely helped that there were no closed windows or doors and the storm blew through the building."

"Good," Gabriel replied.

"Did you find any actual meth?" Jordon asked.

Mark grinned. "Enough to keep Billy cooking up slop in prison for a very long time."

"One more bad apple off the streets," Jordon replied.

"We'll just let you finish up." Gabriel touched her arm. "Let's go check in with Ted and Joan."

She followed behind Gabriel as they headed inside. She couldn't help but think about how nice it had been to have his arms around her through the night, how comfortable she felt with him. Their conversations were so easy, as if they'd known each other for months instead of days. She didn't feel the need to censor herself with him. She trusted that she could just be herself and that was okay with him.

She'd misjudged him at first impression. He wasn't inflexible; he was determined. He wasn't uptight—he was focused, and he was so much more than those things. He was intelligent and could be funny. More important, he seemed to *get* her.

Maybe she was just feeling particularly soft about him because he'd thrown her to the ground and covered her body with his own when the bullets had flown. His first instinct hadn't been to get to cover himself, but rather to protect her.

Not that any of that mattered. She tamped down a strange wistfulness that tried to take hold of her as they entered the main dining room.

Ted sat on one of the chairs by the fireplace and Joan sat at one of the tables. There was an underlying thrum of tension in the air. Joan stood as they entered and worried her hands together.

"We didn't know," she said. Her blue eyes were darker than Jordon had ever seen them. "You have to believe me—we had no idea what Billy was doing out there in the shed."

"A meth lab...murder," Ted said in disgust and gazed at his wife. "All of it happening right here where we live with our children. This would have never happened if we'd stayed in Oklahoma City, where we belonged."

It was obvious the crimes were fracturing what Jordon had presumed was a good and loving relationship.

"Sit down, Joan," Gabriel said calmly. "Nobody believes that you and Ted had anything to do with Billy's meth business."

Jordon walked over to the coffeepot to get a cup of the hot brew while Gabriel took a seat next to Joan.

"How long has this been going on? How long has Billy been cooking drugs on this property?" Ted asked, his voice almost a growl.

Jordon sat at the table next to Gabriel and faced the fireplace and Ted. A rich anger radiated from the man, an anger that appeared to be pointed not only at the circumstances, but also specifically at his wife.

"I checked that shed when Samantha Kent was killed in the woods and there was nothing there. According to what Billy told us, he started just after Christmas when he found out his sister had cancer and needed money," Gabriel said.

"Did he kill those people?" Ted asked. "Is he the killer who is trying to destroy us?"

"We don't believe so," Jordon said.

Ted frowned. "So, we still have a killer running loose around here." He shook his head and gazed at Joan once again. "Happy wife, happy life—yeah, right." He got up from his chair and slammed his coffee cup down on the table. "I've got work to do in the office."

"I'm sorry," Joan said as soon as he'd left the room. "He's upset. We're both upset. This has all been so difficult." She looked utterly miserable as the glint of tears shone in her eyes.

"Don't worry—we understand," Jordon said softly.

"Has Ed come in yet?" Gabriel asked.

"He arrived just a few minutes before you did." She glanced at Jordon. "I sent him right to your room to take care of the window issue."

Gabriel stood. "We'll go check out the progress."

Jordon took a big gulp of her coffee and then got up, as well. "Joan, stay strong. We're going to get this all taken care of."

"I hope so. I was the one who insisted we make this move. Ted really only did it to make me happy." Her hand trembled as she reached up and tucked a strand of hair behind her ear. "I just want this to all go away so we can live the dreams we had."

"We'll do everything we can to make that happen, Joan," Gabriel replied.

"Tensions are definitely rising," Jordon said once they were on the path to her room. "I hate to see what's happening between Joan and Ted."

"Collateral damage," Gabriel replied. "There

are always more victims than the dead ones when something like this happens."

"The ripple effect," she replied. Her stomach clenched. "I want to get this guy so badly I can taste it."

"Speaking of tasting it, we'll stop and get lunch after we leave here and before we start interviewing anyone."

Jordon glanced at her cell phone, shocked to see that it was already almost three. It was amazing how a chase in the woods and an interview with a drug dealer could eat up the hours of the day.

The door to her room was unlocked and they walked in to find Ed in the bathroom installing a new window lock. "I put up a new screen and this should take just a minute," he said after their initial greetings. "I told Ted a month ago that this lock had an issue, but with everything else going on around here, I guess we both forgot about it."

He finished using his screwdriver and then opened the window and tried the new latch several times. "That should do it," he said.

"Just a minute, Ed," Gabriel said before the handyman could leave the suite. "We have a few questions to ask you."

"Questions about what?"

"Where were you last night?"

Ed looked at them in surprise. "I was at home. In fact, Kevin and Glen came over and wound up spending the night. We played cards and drank some beer, and this morning Millie made us all sausage and French toast with my favorite strawberry syrup."

Jordon stared at the man with a rising frustration. She still couldn't be certain if he was off the hook for being the man who had attacked her, but how convenient that he'd just provided an alibi not only for himself but also for his brothers.

"Is there anything else?" Ed asked with his usual pleasantness. "I've got some other work to attend to around here."

"That should do it," Gabriel replied. Once Ed was out the door, Gabriel turned and looked at Jordon. "We'll grab some lunch and then I think it's time we talked to Millie."

"Do you really think she'll say anything different than what Ed told us?"

"Doubtful, but maybe we'll see something in the house that will tell us something different."

"If you don't mind, I'd rather talk to her first and grab lunch afterward," Jordon said. She wanted to tie up any loose ends that they could from the attack the night before as soon as possible.

He shrugged. "Fine by me."

"Will she even let us in the front door?" Jordon asked as they left her room.

He flashed her a quick smile. "It would be downright rude to keep people standing on the front porch on a cold winter's day."

"And Branson is known for its down-home friendliness," she replied.

Why couldn't she get Gabriel's *friendliness* out of her brain? Throughout the interview with Billy, she'd flashed back to the night before and the intimate moments with Gabriel. When they'd entered the room to find Ed, her gaze had shot to the bed where they'd made love the night before.

He'd somehow managed to get under her skin in a way no man had done since Jack. She'd hoped never again to feel the wild electricity, the slight flutter in her heart, for any man. As crazy as it sounded, when she left here the chief of police would have more than just a little bit of her guarded heart.

She mentally shook herself and realized there was an unsettled piece of her brain, as if she'd forgotten something important. But, try as she might, she couldn't figure out what it was, like having a snatch of a lyric to a song going around and around in her head and she couldn't quite remember the title.

Gabriel pulled down a narrow road that thankfully had been plowed earlier in the day. The houses were small and set far apart.

"Unfortunately, Ed's house is fairly isolated and the last place before a dead end. It's doubtful that anyone in the neighborhood would know whether Kevin's and Glen's cars were parked there overnight or not."

Jordon released a deep sigh. "A dead end is where we're at. Nothing is coming easy with this case. I can't go back to Kansas City without this being solved. It would totally ruin my reputation."

"And what reputation is that?" he asked.

"My kick-ass-and-get-it-done reputation," she replied.

He cast her another one of his charming grins. "I certainly wouldn't want to mess with that reputation, so that means we need to kick ass and really get it done."

"Amen," she replied.

He parked in front of a little house painted a dreary brown with a bright red front door. Unfortunately, the driveway was completely shoveled, making it impossible to see whether one car or three cars had been parked there overnight.

She definitely hoped an answer was inside. She not only wanted to catch this guy sooner rather than later, but she also needed to get back to Kansas City before Gabriel dug any deeper into her heart.

MILLIE ROLLINGS WAS a painfully thin woman with mousy brown hair and faded blue eyes that gazed at them warily as she ushered them into a small neat living room that smelled of lemon furniture wax and old coffee.

Gabriel had never had much to do with Ed's wife, whom he saw only occasionally at the grocery store. He'd always gotten the impression of a nervous little bird, and as he introduced her to Jordon, his impression of Millie didn't change.

"Ed told me there was a pretty FBI lady staying at Diamond Cove," she said and self-consciously reached up to touch a strand of her limp hair.

"Do you mind if we have a seat and ask you a few questions?" he asked.

"Of course, please, although I can't imagine what you would want to ask me." She gestured toward the sofa and sat in a chair opposite them.

"We spoke with Ed earlier and he mentioned you had houseguests last night," Jordon said. "Is that correct?"

"Yes. Ed's brothers came by to play cards

and got snowed in until this morning. I made them a big breakfast of sausage and French toast and the strawberry syrup that's Ed's favorite." She reached a hand up once again to pat her hair and her gaze shifted slightly above Jordon's head.

Interesting that she'd used almost the precise same words that Ed had used when he'd described the morning meal. Gabriel would love to get a look at her phone to see how quickly Ed might have called his wife after they'd spoken to him.

"You do realize we're searching for the person who has killed three people in cold blood. If you know anything about these crimes or if you're lying about Kevin and Glen being here last night, you could go to prison for a long time," Gabriel said.

Millie shot back in her chair as if he'd physically struck her. Her lower lip trembled slightly, and this time when she reached up to her hair, she grabbed a strand of it and twirled furiously.

"I'm not a liar. I'm not," she replied. "I'd never risk going to prison for anyone, especially the likes of those two. Me and Ed, we're good people."

"Sometimes good people make mistakes

when it comes to protecting their family," Jordon said softly.

"I wouldn't do that and now I think it's time you both leave." She stood and looked at them expectantly...and defiantly.

The mouse had roared, Gabriel thought. He didn't know whether to be amused or ticked off. He and Jordon rose from the sofa.

"Mrs. Rollings, if you know anything about these murders, anything at all, now is the time to speak up," Jordon said.

"I can't help you and if you have any more questions you talk to Ed." She opened the front door. "Now, please go."

"What do you think?" Jordon asked when they were back in the car.

"I honestly don't know what to think." He started the engine and then pulled away from the house. "She might be telling the truth and she might be lying."

"Have you heard any rumors about her being an abused wife? Is it possible that she's scared of her husband and so would say anything to us that he told her to say?"

"I haven't heard any whispers of abuse," he replied. "But you never know what goes on behind closed doors."

"True. Maybe we should check with the neighbors. Maybe somebody saw or didn't see the cars here that would either prove Millie truthful or a liar."

It took them almost an hour to check with the other people who lived on the same street as Ed Rollings. Unfortunately, it had been a night where most people had hunkered down and weren't paying attention to what their neighbors were doing.

"Now I need to eat," Jordon said as they drove back toward the main strip. "Breakfast seems like it was served a lifetime ago."

"What sounds good?" he asked. Another night in her bed sounded good. Another night of holding her sweet, soft body against his sounded great. "How about a juicy steak?" He hoped his voice didn't betray his physical frustration.

"Hmm, perfect," she replied.

It was almost six when they pulled into a popular steak house where Gabriel often ate. There were only two cars parked in front of the building despite the dinner hour.

As they got out of the car, Gabriel was struck by a bone-weariness. Between the trauma of the night before, the shoot-out with Billy and all the other events that had occurred within the past twenty-four hours, it was no wonder he was tired.

This case was eating him alive, and when

he wasn't thinking about murder, he was thinking far too much about Jordon. Before he'd gone to sleep the night before, he'd been determined to put a little distance between himself and his partner. However, they'd shared another bout of lovemaking in the middle of the night, and so far the distance he'd thought he'd be able to maintain wasn't happening. Hell, he wanted her again right this minute.

The owner of the restaurant, Bob Carson, greeted them at the door. "Slow night with the weather, Chief. You've pretty much got your pick of tables or booths." He held out two menus.

"Thanks, Bob." Gabriel took the menus and then led Jordon to a booth toward the back of the restaurant. There was only one other couple seated at a table in the same general area.

They had just gotten situated and peered at the menus when Bob appeared at the booth with an order pad. "My waitresses didn't show up tonight due to the snow."

"Does this mean you'll also be cooking our meals?" Gabriel asked with a touch of humor.

Bob laughed. "No. You're in luck—the chef actually made it in along with one busboy. Now, what can I get for you two this evening?"

Jordon ordered a strip steak and a loaded baked potato and Gabriel got the rib eye with creamy mashed potatoes. They both ordered soft drinks and then Jordon leaned against the high, red leather booth back.

She looked achingly beautiful but her eyes appeared tired and slightly hollow.

"You look exhausted," he said softly.

"I am," she admitted.

"I think we've done enough today. After we eat I'll take you back to your room, unless you're finally ready to agree to get a room at another motel," he said, desperately wishing she would agree to go someplace safe.

She laughed, the slightly husky sound that stirred him on all levels, and shook her head. "You're nothing if not consistent, Chief Walters."

"Jordon, I care about your safety," he replied.

"I care about my safety, too, but that doesn't mean I'm going to run and hide. Ed fixed the window lock, and if it makes you feel better then you can walk me to my door each night and check the room before I settle in."

"Do you have some sort of a death wish?"

"Of course not," she replied quickly. "I'll

admit I take some risks, but they're always calculated ones."

Their conversation was interrupted by the arrival of their meals. Unlike most of the meals they had shared, Jordon was unusually silent and appeared distracted.

Gabriel didn't know if it was because she was tired or if he might have made her angry with his death-wish question. Although he would have liked to prod her into telling him more about herself, about her current mood, instead he gave her space and remained quiet.

They were halfway through the meal when she placed her fork down and stared at him thoughtfully. "Something has been bothering me all afternoon and I finally figured out what it was."

"What's that?" he asked curiously.

"Ted."

Gabriel looked at her in surprise. "What about him?"

"I'm just wondering how hard Joan really had to twist his arm to move here." Her eyes darkened slightly. "I'm wondering what lengths he might go to in order to get back to life in Oklahoma City."

Gabriel sucked in a deep breath. Was it even possible? Would Ted sabotage the family business by killing three people in cold blood to ruin his wife's dream and get her and their children back where he thought they belonged?

"That's sick and it's crazy," he finally said.

"I know, right?" she replied. "But we knew we might be chasing crazy. Ted lives right across the street. He'd have access and intimate knowledge of the area."

"But he had a solid alibi for Samantha Kent's murder. He was having breakfast in the dining room with other people when she was killed," Gabriel protested.

"The medical examiner only has to be wrong about the time of the attack by twenty minutes or so. That would have given Ted time to stab her, clean himself up and appear for breakfast."

She leaned forward, her eyes blazing with the spark of life that had been missing before. "Ed mentioned that he'd told Ted about the window lock not working a month ago and yet he put me in that very room. Why not one of the other empty rooms? I know we checked into their backgrounds, but we were looking at it from the viewpoint that they were victims. I'm just saying maybe we need to approach an investigation into Ted from a new angle."

She picked up her fork once again and Gabriel set his down, his appetite gone as he realized they had managed to take one suspect off their list but had just added another one.

Chapter Ten

Another week passed far too slowly. The cases had all gone cold, and although the investigation continued, they were grasping at straws. One of the only good things that had happened was the weather had warmed up and the snow had finally melted away.

Jordon now sat in the conference room alone. Gabriel was attending to other duties in his office and she'd been reading through the interviews and the background material they'd gathered throughout the past week.

They'd spoken to Glen's, Ed's and Kevin's neighbors and friends in an effort to get a handle on the three brothers who topped their list of suspects.

They'd also spent hours on the phone speaking to anyone they could find who had been in Ted's and Joan's lives in Oklahoma City before they'd bought the Diamond Cove.

This time the investigation wasn't seeking to find somebody who was an enemy of the couple.

Much of their efforts had been focused on digging into Ted's past to see if there was any indication that he harbored a dark and twisted soul. He had no criminal record other than a speeding ticket he'd received four years ago.

They'd spoken with former coworkers, and Jordon had spent hours digging into social media where he was fairly active. She'd studied his posts and stared at his photos for so long he invaded her dreams, but she'd found nothing out of the ordinary.

She'd not only delved into Ted's social media, but had also looked at Joan's. She'd even been desperate enough to study Jason's and Hannah's online presences, figuring sometimes children might share something about family tension.

Joan had posted fairly regularly when she'd been a teacher but had apparently put her blogging efforts into the official Diamond Cove website when they'd moved here. Her cheerful, inviting blogs had fallen off after the first murder.

Jason posted irregularly, mostly sharing things that teenage guys would find interesting. He had been unhappy about the move and talked about leaving his friends, but later posts indicated that he'd adjusted okay and had made new friends. Hannah had little social media, which was rather surprising for a fifteen-year-old girl.

Jordon sighed and cast her gaze out the nearby window where dusk was just beginning to paint the world in deep purple shadows. Another night nearly gone and they weren't any closer to solving the case.

However, she had definitely grown closer to her partner. He invaded her dreams, as well. They were not just sizzling erotic dreams, but also sweet and filled with all kinds of wonderful that she knew she'd never have in her real life.

She'd grown to care about him deeply and she had a feeling he was feeling the same way about her. That only made her need to solve this case more pressing than ever.

Even though they'd known each other for only a little over two weeks, they had probably spent more time together than most couples who had been married for six months or so.

They'd learned each other's little quirks. She knew he liked his burgers without ketchup and with extra mayo and that he refused to drink cold coffee. His energy level fell somewhat in the late afternoons, but he got a second wind after eating dinner.

Those were just the superficial things she'd discovered about him. She'd also learned he had a kind heart, that he had a secret passion for supporting animal rights and that his eyes softened and lightened in hue whenever he gazed at her.

The very last thing she wanted to do was break his heart. He was such a good man and he deserved a good woman. As much as she'd like to think otherwise, that woman would never, ever be her.

A wave of loneliness, of quiet sorrow struck her, piercing through her heart and bringing an unexpected sting of tears to her eyes.

She'd once had such dreams of sharing her life with a special man. She'd once believed she'd have a husband who would be her soft place to fall, a man who would be by her side until death. But those dreams had been stolen and she refused to believe in anything like that ever again.

This case was definitely not only getting to her on a professional level, but also on a personal one. Angrily she swiped at her eyes and sat up straighter in the chair. She was good alone. That was the way it was supposed to be and there was no sense getting all teary-eyed about it.

The conference room door opened and Gabriel swept in, filling the room with his solid presence, with his male vitality. "Now, where were we?" he asked.

She shoved the files away. "At the same dead end we were at a week ago," she replied with an uncharacteristic pessimism darkening her tone. "It would be nice if we could just identify somebody with the means and a clear motive, but I'm beginning to wonder if any of our suspects are really good for these murders." She released a heavy sigh.

He frowned. "That doesn't sound like the kick-butt partner I've come to know and love."

"I guess I'm just not feeling it right now," she replied.

"Has all work and no play made Agent James a grumpy woman?"

"Possibly," she admitted.

"My recommendation is we grab our coats, get out of here and go someplace where we can kick back and have a couple of drinks," he replied.

She immediately stood and pulled her coat from the back of her chair. "Just lead me to the nearest bar."

He grinned at her. "Now, that's the go-get-'em spirit."

Fifteen minutes later he pulled up in front of a small tavern off the main drag. A wooden sign across the doorway proclaimed the place to be Joe's.

"I know, it's a bit of a dive, but it's my favorite place to come and unwind," he said as he turned off the car. "The music is low, the drinks are good and strong, and here nobody expects anything from me except that I pay the tab before I leave."

"Sounds like the perfect place to end a fairly depressing day," she replied.

They got out of the car and he ushered her inside with his hand in the middle of her back. It was just one of many of the casual touches they'd shared since the night they'd made love, but tonight she felt particularly vulnerable and it affected her more deeply than ever before.

Joe's held a long polished bar with a dozen stools. Two men sat on opposite sides of the bar and an older man with a graying beard stood behind it and nodded in greeting to them as they entered.

Gabriel led her to one of the handful of booths where a small bowl of peanuts was the centerpiece. A country song about lost love and a broken heart played on speakers overhead. Jordon took off her coat and then slid into the black leather booth.

"What can I get for you?" Gabriel asked her.

She frowned thoughtfully. "A gin and tonic with a twist of lime," she finally replied. She didn't want a civilized glass of wine. She wanted…needed something stronger to take the edge off her uncharacteristic blue mood.

She watched Gabriel as he walked to the bar. It wasn't her growing feelings for him that had her so discouraged. It wasn't, she told herself firmly.

The real problem was that she was afraid she'd be called back to Kansas City before they caught the bad guy. The job was the only successful part of her life, and she was afraid she'd leave here as a failure, and she'd already been a failure in so many other areas of her life.

He returned to the booth with their drinks and sat across from her. "What is your poison tonight?" she asked.

"Scotch and soda. My father introduced me to the pleasure of fine scotch when I got old enough to have an occasional drink with him."

"You're close to your parents?"

"Very," he replied. "They moved from Chicago to Florida several years ago, but they come up to visit me at least once a year and we stay in touch by phone."

"They must be very proud of you," she replied.

He smiled. "They are, but I think they'd be proud of me no matter what I chose to do for a living."

The front door opened and she glanced over to see Glen Rollings come in. The relaxation that had been about to take over her came to a screeching halt as every muscle in her body tensed.

Gabriel followed her gaze and muttered a small curse under his breath. "What in the hell is he doing here?"

Glen ambled over to their booth with a wide smile. "What a small world. Chief Walters, I didn't know we shared the same drinking hole. I was just driving by here and saw your car and thought I'd stop in to say hello." He winked at Jordon. "Figured I'd take the chance at seeing the hottest woman in town one more time."

"Hello and goodbye," Jordon replied, not attempting to mask her irritation.

"Move it along, Glen. We're busy here," Gabriel said, his eyes narrowed as he glared at the blond-haired man.

"Jeez, you guys don't have to be so unfriendly," Glen replied.

"We're both not feeling too friendly right now," Jordon said.

"Wow. Okay, then. I guess I'll just see you later." Glen turned around and headed for the bar, where he sat on one of the stools.

"In all the times I've been here, I've never seen any of the Rollings brothers," Gabriel said. "I don't like this sudden appearance."

Jordon cast Glen another glance. He had a beer in front of him and was half-turned on the stool so that he could see them. She looked back at Gabriel. "Do you think he followed us here?"

"I don't know. Maybe he is a regular here and I've just never seen him." He took a drink and then grabbed a handful of peanuts. "Just ignore him."

For a few minutes they sat silently. Jordon felt Glen's steady gaze on her, making it impossible for her to just ignore him as Gabriel had advised.

Was he their man? Was it possible he had seen the car outside and wondered if maybe she was inside here by herself? Alone and vulnerable?

All the other murders had taken place on Diamond Cove property, but that didn't mean the next one would. The killer could always change up his game. Maybe for him it was enough that she was a "guest" at the resort.

Thankfully, Glen finished his beer fairly quickly and then left. It was only then that her muscles began to slowly unknot. "That was weird," she said.

"Maybe it wasn't as weird as it felt. It's possible he really did see the car and maybe thought he could charm you. I think he has a crush on you."

Jordon was somehow grateful that Gabriel's thoughts about the situation hadn't gone as dark as hers had. She sat up straighter in the seat and picked up some peanuts.

"Tell me about your parents," he said. "You've heard all about mine, but you never mention yours."

"That's because we aren't real close. My mother and father own a successful law firm back in Denver. They're both defense lawyers who specialize in high-profile cases. They wanted me to follow in their footsteps and work at the firm, but that wasn't the side of the law I wanted to work."

"They were unhappy with your decision to become an FBI agent?"

An old pain attempted to grab hold of her, but she shoved it away. She'd long ago made peace with the fact that she hadn't been the daughter her parents had wanted.

"They weren't happy about my career choice and they weren't happy that I never had an interest to rub shoulders with their society friends." She smiled at him wryly. "I think they were probably disappointed that I had curly dark hair instead of beautiful gleaming blond tresses, too."

"I love your hair," he replied. "And I love that you're an FBI agent and here with me right now." His eyes gleamed in the low lighting.

"Thanks." She grabbed some of the peanuts, aware that his gaze was a little too soft and filled with a lot of inviting heat.

"So, what are some other places where you hang out in your downtime?" she asked, determined to steer the conversation onto a lighter topic.

"I occasionally go to the local animal shelter and play with the dogs."

"Why don't you have one?" she asked curiously. "You know, man's best friend and all that."

"My lifestyle wouldn't be good for a dog. I work long hours and it wouldn't be fair."

"Working long hours makes any kind of a relationship difficult," she replied.

He nodded. "People who aren't in the life don't understand the drive, the passion we feel for this work." He cocked his head to the side and gazed at her curiously. "Was that an issue in your marriage?"

"Not really. Jack loved the fact that I sometimes worked long hours. It gave him an opportunity to cheat with women who were better than me." She looked down into her empty glass, shocked that she'd spilled this particular piece of her past.

"Better than you? What in the hell does that mean?"

She looked up to see his intense gaze boring into her. "Can I get another drink?"

He held her gaze for another long moment and then got up from the booth and headed for the bar. Jeez, what had made her dredge up the failures of her marriage? With the arrival of Glen and now the conversation, this downtime definitely wasn't as refreshing as she'd expected when they'd left the station.

As she stared at Gabriel's back, she knew the answer as to why she'd brought up her marriage. She had to remind herself that she wasn't fit to be a wife, that she wasn't good for any real relationship. Something about the way Gabriel watched her made her want to believe differently about herself, but she knew the truth and she had to cling to it.

He returned to the booth with her drink. "Now, tell me all about this creep that you married."

She took a big swallow of her gin. "He wasn't a creep," she said as she set her glass down. "I met Jack at a charity function. He owned an insurance company and was a well-respected figure in the community. He was handsome and smart and charming, and I fell hard for him. We dated for eight months and then got married."

She'd been so happy, so certain that she'd found her soul mate. Even her parents, who had never been particularly pleased with anything she did, had approved of Jack.

"We had a blissful couple of months before the cracks started to appear," she said. "He thought I was messy, so I tried really hard to keep things neat and tidy. He didn't like my jokes and so I tried to be more serious. The first year was definitely an adjustment for us. And then I heard from a mutual friend that he was seeing another woman."

It was an old hurt that had scabbed over long ago, but as she remembered that time, she was surprised to realize it still hurt just a little bit.

"Did you confront him?" Gabriel asked softly.

She nodded. "I did, and he confessed that he'd met her a few times for drinks and that was all there was to it. He swore he wouldn't see her again, that he wanted our marriage to work, and I believed him."

"And so the marriage continued."

"I didn't want another failure. Marrying Jack was the one thing I'd done that my parents approved of, so I was desperate to make it work. Then I found some sexy text messages on his phone that made it clear he was having an affair, and yes, I was snooping."

She took another big gulp of her drink and realized she was more than a little bit buzzed. She'd always been a lightweight when it came to hard liquor.

She offered Gabriel a rueful smile. "The problem wasn't Jack—it was me. I didn't know how to make him happy. I didn't know how to be a partner. I'm just not good wife material."

"That's not true." His eyes filled with a warmth that washed over her. "You just weren't Jack's wife material and I still think he's a creep."

She laughed. "Partners are supposed to be loyal to each other. I promise I'll hate anyone who breaks your heart, and now I think it's time for me to get back to my room for the night."

They got up and pulled their coats on, and Jordon stood by the door while Gabriel paid the tab. When he ushered her outside, a deep scowl possessed his features.

"What's wrong?" she asked him once they were in the car.

He buckled his seat belt and then turned to look at her, his eyes so dark she fought against an inner shiver. "Joe just told me that he'd never seen Glen in the bar before tonight."

All the black thoughts she'd momentarily entertained when Glen had sat on the bar stool staring at her rushed back into her head.

"He implied to us that he was a regular customer," she said.

Gabriel pulled out on the road to take her back to the bed-and-breakfast. "I don't know if he's a real threat or if he just really drove by and saw the patrol car like he said. We know for sure now that he's a liar."

Jordon leaned her head back and closed her eyes. The travel back to her broken marriage, coupled with the new concern of a stalking

Glen, swept away any pleasant buzz the alcohol might have given her.

She turned in her seat and glanced behind them, but no cars shared the secondary road with them.

"Don't worry. I'm watching, too," Gabriel said.

"I just don't understand these men. It's like Kevin and Glen are intentionally doing things to make them look like suspects. Are they just stupid or are they that calculating and they're trying to muddy things up for us?"

"Neither of them are rocket-scientist material, but they are cunning. I'll call Mark and have him assign somebody to keep an eye on Glen. I want to know what he's doing and when he's doing it."

"Sounds like a plan," she replied.

"I'm sorry the night ended up like this. I was hoping we'd both relax and kick back a bit."

"It's not your fault Glen showed up and ruined the mood."

It took only minutes to arrive back at Diamond Cove. They both got out of the car and walked up the path to her room, guided through the dark night by the solar lights.

Gabriel pulled his gun as she unlocked her

door. This had become their routine since the night she'd been attacked.

She opened the door and they both went inside fast. Immediately he went to the bathroom, where she knew he'd check to make sure nobody was hiding and that the window remained securely locked.

She checked in the closet and under the bed, and when the room was cleared, he sat in the chair next to the fireplace and she sat on the edge of the bed facing him.

"Looks like I'm good for another night," she said.

He nodded, his eyes holding a gleam of hunger. "Jordon, about your marriage… The only mistake you made was not marrying a man who loved your sense of humor, a man who didn't care about housekeeping or cooking and such nonsense. You just need to be with a man who understands you and loves you just the way you are."

She jumped up from the bed, afraid that he was going to say something stupid, afraid that she would fall for his sweet words and ultimately he'd only wind up being another person she disappointed.

"I'm tired, Gabriel. I don't want to talk anymore about my past or Glen Rollings or murder or anything else." She stood by the door. "I just need to get some sleep."

He got up from the chair and joined her at the door. "Then I guess I'll just say goodnight." There was a wistfulness in his tone that held the promise of the warmth of his arms, the heat of his body against hers.

She could have him if she wanted him for the night. All she had to do was ask him to stay and she knew he would. The idea was definitely tempting, but she steeled her heart.

"Good night, Gabriel," she said and opened the door.

He stepped outside and then turned to look at her. "You know I'm more than just a little bit crazy over you."

Her heart squeezed tight. "Get over it," she replied forcefully. "I've never lived up to anyone's expectations, Gabriel, and I certainly wouldn't live up to yours."

She closed the door before he could respond and leaned her head against the wood. She wished he'd never told her what he felt about her. She wished he was the antagonistic bonehead she'd initially thought he was going to be.

Instead he was a man she could love, a man who could fill the empty spaces of her life.

But she refused to love him. She cared about him too much to fall into a rosy glow with him that would only end in flames of regret.

Chapter Eleven

He'd wanted her tonight. He'd wanted to hold her in his arms and make love to her. He'd needed to somehow erase whatever insecurities her ex-husband had scarred into her soul. Although she hadn't gone into great detail, she'd said enough to let Gabriel know that the marriage had wounded her in a way to make her believe she was unworthy.

Instead of going home, Gabriel returned to the station, thoughts of the conversation they'd shared in the bar still haunting him. She had so much to offer a man who captured her heart, but she didn't believe she had anything to give.

There was no question that she'd rebuffed him tonight. She'd shoved him out of the door as if he was the devil himself. He didn't know what to do with the feelings he had for her, but it was obvious she had no interest in them.

He parked in front of the station and went inside, unsurprised to find Mark working at his desk. "You know we don't pay overtime," he said and sank in the chair across from Mark.

Mark smiled. "Sheila flew out this morning to spend a couple of weeks with her parents. The house was so quiet without her I decided to come in and catch up on some paperwork. What are you doing here so late? I thought you and Agent James had knocked off for the day."

"We had," Gabriel replied and then told Mark about Glen showing up at the bar. "I want a tail put on him. I don't know what his game is, but I don't like it. Him showing up at Joe's just didn't feel right."

"I'll take care of it," Mark replied. "I'll talk to Ben before I leave here. You know how good he and his team are at undercover surveillance."

Gabriel nodded and released a deep sigh. Ben Hammond ran a private investigation agency in town and was often tapped to help out the small police department.

"This is a tough one," Mark said.

Gabriel didn't have to ask him what he was talking about. Mark had been part of the team of officers working alongside Gabriel and Jordon on the cases.

"I thought when I left Chicago behind I was also leaving behind these kind of tough cases," Gabriel said.

"You probably also thought you'd be working for a mayor who was a normal, rational human being," Mark said wryly. "He's thrown us all under the bus in his last couple of news conferences."

Gabriel leaned back. "We're all busting our butts to solve this case and he's whining about our lack of progress." He shook his head ruefully.

"How's Agent James holding up?"

"Like all the rest of us she's frustrated and weary." And she'd never lived up to anyone's expectations. Gabriel frowned as her parting words played in his head. Something about the funny, brash Agent Jordon James broke his heart just a little bit.

"She's a tough one," Mark said.

"She is," Gabriel agreed.

"I heard from the grapevine that Ted Overton has been spending a lot of time alone in some local watering holes lately," Mark said.

Gabriel frowned thoughtfully. "Wish I knew if he's trying to drown his guilt or just drinking his misery away."

"I don't know, but from all my sources he's definitely trying to drown something."

Gabriel stood abruptly and released a weary sigh. "Go home, Mark. Get a good night's sleep."

"And you do the same," Mark replied, although he made no move to get out of his chair.

A few minutes later Gabriel was back in his car, but he wasn't heading home. He wouldn't rest easy unless he knew exactly where Glen Rollings was right now. He needed to make sure the man wasn't parked down the street from Diamond Cove and potentially planning some sort of an attack on Jordon.

Glen lived not too far from Ed, but unlike Ed's small neat house, Glen's place was a tiny cabin that appeared not to have enjoyed any outside maintenance for the last twenty years or so.

The window shutters had either fallen off or hung by a single nail, and it was impossible to tell what color the cabin might have once been painted, for it had weathered to a dull gray.

Gabriel breathed a sigh of relief as he saw Glen's car parked outside and lights beaming out from the windows. He pulled to a stop just past the house and called Mark.

"I just wanted to let you know that Glen Rollings's current location is his home. I thought you might want to tell Ben that when you speak to him."

"I already talked to him. I gave him Glen's address and he's going to have somebody in place within the next half hour."

"Thanks, Mark. I appreciate it."

The two men hung up and Gabriel left, this time heading for home. If he couldn't put a man on Jordon, then this was the next best thing. He would have liked to put a tail on all their suspects, but it simply wasn't financially feasible. Glen's appearance in the bar had been odd and unsettling enough that he could justify the expense of a tail. Although he was certain that Mayor Donald Stoddard would bitch and moan about the use of the private agency.

I've never lived up to anyone's expectations.

Jordon's words haunted him as he entered his house and as he undressed and got into bed. She'd far exceeded his expectations of her professionally, and she'd also exceeded his expectations of her as a desirable, exciting woman.

He fell into a troubled sleep filled with images of a shadowy person with a wicked-looking knife chasing Jordon through the woods. He ran after them, desperate to help her, but the trees all came to life, their limbs grabbing at him to hold him back.

It was just after seven the next morning when he walked into the Diamond Cove dining room, where Jordon and Joan were already seated at a table.

Joan looked haggard and as if she hadn't slept in days. The pleasant sparkle that normally lit her eyes was gone, replaced by the dark pall this case had cast over everyone involved.

Joan and Jordon greeted him before Joan jumped up from the table and hurried into the kitchen. "Everything all right?" he asked after he'd poured a cup of coffee and sunk down in the chair opposite Jordon.

After the conversation they'd had the night before, he wasn't sure what kind of mood to expect from her this morning. "According to Joan, Ted is drinking too much, the kids are starting to act out and she feels like her entire world is falling apart." Her eyes sparked with anger. "This case is really ticking me off."

"We can only chase what leads we get, and right now there aren't any to chase," Gabriel replied. "We've now got a tail on Glen, so if he's our man and he makes a move, we'll be on him before anyone else gets hurt."

"And if he isn't our man?" She raised one of her eyebrows.

Gabriel frowned. "Then we'll find the person who is our man. I don't know what else to say." He still couldn't quite gauge her mood.

"I know you don't. I'm just frustrated." She released a deep sigh. "Maybe I just need to make myself a bigger target. I need to appear as more vulnerable bait. I could spend the nights sitting in a rocking chair outside of my room…or maybe…"

"Stop." Gabriel interrupted her in horror and leaned forward in his chair. "You aren't going to do anything like that."

"You're right—I'm not. I just wish this creep would make another move." She took a sip of her coffee and then set the cup back down on the table. "You know I can't stay here forever." Her gaze held his intently and then she stared down into her coffee cup.

"Do you know how much longer we've got with you here?" His heart suddenly felt too big for his chest and he had to talk around a lump that rose up in his throat.

He'd known she was here only temporarily, but in the past week or so he'd somehow buried that fact deep in his mind. It had been easier to not think about the time she'd have to go.

"I spoke to my director last night and he's giving me another two weeks and then it's time for me to go back home," she replied.

"Here we are," Joan said as she entered the dining room carrying two plates of scrambled eggs, toasted English muffins and strips of crispy bacon.

Two weeks. It wasn't a lot of time. Gabriel picked up his fork even though his appetite had fled. They had fourteen days to catch the killer.

And he had two weeks to try to stop falling deeper in love with her.

JORDON SAT IN the center of her bed and stared at her laptop monitor. It was just after nine and the frustration of another fruitless day burned hot in her belly.

That wasn't all that burned inside her. She was in love with Gabriel and she wished he was beside her right now, in her bed…in her life forever.

The night that they'd slept together she'd thought he would just be a fling, a warm memory for her to embrace on lonely nights. Gabriel in her bed had been exciting and wonderful, but Gabriel out of her bed was everything she had ever wanted, everything she had ever dreamed of in a man.

But she knew he wouldn't settle for anything less than marriage and she wasn't willing to go through that again. He was terrific husband material and she was nothing more than mistress material. And to believe anything otherwise would be a disservice to them both.

With a deep frown, she got up from the bed, refusing to think about all the things she wouldn't allow in her life. She knew who and what she was, and whether Gabriel knew it or not, he deserved much better.

She'd almost been grateful when Director Langford had told her he was pulling her off the case after another two weeks. All she had to do was hang on to her heart and remember she was a lone wolf for the next fourteen days.

What she needed now was a cup of coffee from the guest shed and then a good night's sleep. She wrapped on her gun belt, pulled on her coat and stepped out of her room.

The temperature had dropped again but not before the last couple of warm days had melted the snow left by the night of the blizzard.

As always when she left her room at night,

she kept her hand on the butt of her gun and her senses on high alert. The night was silent around her, but she scanned the area with narrowed eyes.

There was no way she was going to let somebody get a jump on her. She was ready for anything that might come out of the darkness. She would never be taken by surprise again.

She reached the guest shed and opened the door. Instantly every nerve in her body electrified and her muscles tensed. There had been no welcoming tinkle of the bell. In fact, the small silver bell that had hung over the door was gone.

Her breaths became shallow as she yanked her gun from her holster and fell into a crouch. Was he inside here with her, or was he just outside and had hoped she wouldn't notice that the bell was missing.

Was he just waiting for her to turn toward the coffee machine and watch a drink fill a cup and then he'd come at her and stab her in the back like he had Rick Sanders?

She twirled toward the door and then pivoted to face both the laundry room door and then the storage room door. Her heart ticked like a time bomb in her chest. Despite the cold of the night, her fingers grew slick with sweat on the gun handle.

Where was he? She turned sideways so both the laundry room door and the entry into the shed were in her vision. She pulled the laundry room door open and released a frantic gasp of air.

Nobody there.

She refused to give in to the shudders of fear that attempted to possess her. She still had to clear the small storage room and watch her back for anyone coming in from outside.

Heart still racing, she grabbed the storage room door handle, turned it and then kicked the door open. Despite the relative darkness of the room, it was easy to see that nobody was inside.

She whirled to face the door that led back outside. Any desire she might have had for a flavored coffee was gone, vanished by the sick knot of nerves that twisted inside her.

The bell over the door had been there two nights ago when she'd come inside to get coffee. It hadn't just dropped off to the floor and there was absolutely no reason Ted and Joan would have had it removed.

She stepped back outside, her gaze frantically shooting in all directions. She got back safely to her room and sank down on the edge of her bed, and only then did her heartbeat begin to slow.

It was him. The killer had taken down the bell. He was toying with her. Had he been someplace nearby? Watching her search the room? Laughing at her fear?

Her stomach clenched, this time not in fear, but rather in anger. He was so close... so damn close. He had to have known about the bell over the door. He had to know that about every other evening she made the trek to the shed for a late-night cup of coffee.

Had he hoped she wouldn't notice the missing bell? Had he hoped that she'd be unaware enough to go into the shed, stand in front of the coffeemaker and be attacked from behind?

If that was the case then he must think she was stupid. She frowned. And why wouldn't he believe that? They hadn't caught him yet even though apparently he was moving around right under their noses.

She carried her simmering anger with her the next morning into the dining room, where Gabriel was already seated at a table, chatting with Joan.

"Good morning," she said curtly. "The bell

over the door in the guest shed is gone," she added before either of them could reply.

"What do you mean gone?" Joan asked in surprise.

"The bracket is still there but it looks like the bell was torn off." Jordon stalked over to the coffeemaker.

"Who would have done such a thing?" Joan asked.

Jordon turned to look at her.

Joan raised a hand to her mouth. "The killer. He didn't want anyone warned of him coming in behind them."

"Give the little lady a stuffed bear," Jordon replied as she poured herself a cup of coffee. Once she was finished, she walked back to the table and sat across from Gabriel.

He gazed at her with a deep frown. "When exactly did you discover this?"

"Last night it was just after nine when I decided to get myself a cup of coffee from the shed. The minute I stepped through the door I realized the bell hadn't tinkled."

"How often at night are you leaving your room to get coffee?" he asked, his voice holding a wealth of disapproval as his gaze bored into hers.

"I'll just go see to breakfast," Joan said and quickly left the room.

"Every other night or so," Jordon said in response to Gabriel's question.

"Tell me, Agent James—on those nights do you really want a cup of coffee or are you taunting the killer to make a move on you?"

He was definitely angry. As if calling her Agent James wasn't enough to let her know, the deepening frown across his forehead and the taut slash of his lips was a sure sign of his ire.

She smiled at him. "I told you when we first met that if you hung around me long enough you'd get irritated with me."

"This isn't funny, Jordon," he replied. "I have nightmares about something happening to you."

She looked at him in surprise. "You dream about me?"

He shook his head. "Don't change the subject. Answer my question."

"I forgot what the question was."

He leaned back in his chair and released a deep sigh of obvious frustration. "Have you been intentionally taunting the killer to come after you?"

She thoughtfully stared down into her coffee cup and then looked back at him once again. "I don't know," she finally answered truthfully. "I mean, I'm definitely a coffee freak and I like to drink a cup in the evenings, but maybe subconsciously I was hoping the killer would come after me."

"You aren't alone in this. We're a team, Jordon. It's bad enough that you're staying here. The last thing I want is for you to take any additional chances that put you in greater danger." His gaze softened and his mouth relaxed a bit.

"I won't get coffee at night anymore," she said quickly, afraid by the look on his face that he was going to say something stupid... something that might twist her heart.

"That only makes me feel a little better," he replied.

Joan came in with their breakfast plates, thankfully ending that particular conversation. "I'll have Ed hang another bell in the shed as soon as he comes in this morning."

Jordon exchanged a pointed gaze with Gabriel and she knew he was thinking the same thing. It was very possible that the man who would be replacing the bell was the same one who had yanked it off.

Was she mistaken in her belief that her attacker on the night of the snowstorm hadn't been Ed? In retrospect she really couldn't be sure. It had all happened so very fast.

Or had he taken down the bell to clear the

way for one of his brothers to make a move on her? The idea of three of them working in concert was so disturbing.

The day had barely begun and already a dull throb pressed tight across the back of her skull. She had a deadly man to find and a wonderful man to forget.

Chapter Twelve

Ten days.

And tomorrow it would be nine more days and Jordon would be gone. Gabriel turned around at his desk and stared out the nearby window where another day had ended and night had fallen.

When the bell had gone missing in the guest shed, he'd added a tail to both Kevin Rollings and Ted Overton, but over the past couple of days neither one of the men had gone anywhere or done anything suspicious.

Gabriel knew he couldn't justify the tails remaining in place for too long, especially not having any concrete evidence to tie them to the crimes other than Kevin's vocal hatred of Diamond Cove.

A knock on his door turned him around in the chair. Mark entered the office and sank down in the chair in front of his desk. "Another frustrating day, huh," he said. "Maybe the killer is done. Maybe he figures the three murders have already ruined business for Diamond Cove and he's finished."

Gabriel smiled. "Thanks for trying to inject a little optimism into my heart, but we both know he isn't finished." His smile fell. "And right now it appears that we're stuck just waiting for his next move."

"He's marked Agent James as his next victim, but so far he's been unsuccessful in getting to her. Let's just hope he doesn't change his mind and decide to go after somebody else, like a member of the Overton family."

"There's been no indication that the family is at risk, which makes Ted even better as a potential suspect," Gabriel replied. "However, I have warned them all to not be on the property alone, especially at night."

"I know Agent James is leaving town soon. What happens when his target goes away?"

Gabriel's gut tightened, and he didn't know if it was because Jordon would be gone or knowing that the killer would probably find another target.

"I don't know," he finally replied. "I can't stop Ted and Joan from reopening their business and that means any of their guests could be potential victims."

"If they have any guests."

"Oh, they'll have guests. If nothing else they'd get stupid people who want to stay in a place where murder has taken place." Gabriel swallowed against a bit of disgust.

"So, I guess the only thing we can hope for is that our man comes after Agent James within the next week or so," Mark said.

That was the last thing Gabriel hoped would happen. He wanted the killer caught but he didn't want Jordon involved. He was torn between being a chief of police who trusted that an FBI agent could take care of herself, and being a man who wanted nothing more than to protect the woman who held a big chunk of his heart.

"I guess I'm out of here," Mark said and got up from the chair. "I'll see you in the morning."

"Good night, Mark." Gabriel shut down his computer and then stood. It was time to get Jordon back to her suite. He put on his coat, left his office and then walked down to the conference room where she had been working alone for the last hour while Gabriel caught up on all the other crimes in the area.

He opened the conference room door and her fresh, floral scent instantly assaulted his nose. She looked up from whatever she'd been reading and her smile warmed him to his very soul.

"Another day is done," she said. She slid the paper into one of the manila folders on the table and then stood.

"Another day of more dead ends," he replied.

She pulled on her coat. "Don't beat yourself up, Gabriel. We both know we're at a point in the investigation where the ball is in the killer's court."

"Don't remind me," he said drily. "Are you hungry? Want to grab something before I take you back to Diamond Cove?" They had eaten a late lunch, but he'd much prefer the final meal of the day spent with her than alone in his kitchen.

"I'm really not very hungry. I'm good just going to my room," she replied.

He nodded despite his disappointment. She'd been rather distant with him all day. During lunch she'd been quiet, far more introspective than he'd ever seen her. It was as if mentally she was already moving on and putting him and these crimes behind her.

She was quiet as they left the building, got into his car and left the station. "The weather report says more snow coming in sometime tonight," he said to break the silence.

"Hopefully it isn't going to be another blizzard," she replied.

"Nah, right now they're just calling for an inch or two."

"That's good." She stared out the passenger window and the silence resumed.

He tried to think of something inane, any light topic that would draw her out, but the things he really wanted to talk about with her weren't light or inane.

Tonight the depth of his feelings for her begged to be spoken out loud. They filled his heart with a fullness that was difficult to hold in. As crazy as it was, he knew in his very soul that she was the woman he wanted not just for the next ten days, but rather for the rest of his life. And until this moment he'd believed that she was falling in love with him.

They reached Diamond Cove and they both got out of the car. As always, he drew his gun as she unlocked her suite door. Once the room was cleared, they took off their coats and he sat on the chair next to the fireplace.

"How about a cup of coffee before I take off?" he asked.

"Okay, I'll make a pot, although this isn't as good as the flavored ones in the guest shed." She walked over to the vanity where the little coffeepot sat next to a small basket that held coffee packages, creamers and sugar packets.

He watched her covetously as she poured the water into the back of the machine, set the coffee packet inside and then turned it on to brew.

She was so beautiful and seemingly so unaware of her own attractiveness. It wasn't just her physical charm that drew him to her, but also the spirit and beauty that shone from within.

As she turned around to face him, he got up and flipped the switch that made flames jump to life in the fireplace. He sat back down in the chair and knew this night wouldn't end without him speaking exactly what was in his heart.

"Long day," she finally said when the coffee was finished and she'd poured them each a cup. She set hers on the nightstand and moved aside what appeared to be a red nightgown that was on her bed, along with a can of hair product and a tube of mascara, and then sat down.

"They're all long lately," he replied. When he'd worked as a cop in Chicago, he'd once faced down a man high on PCP and armed with a machete. He and his partner had gotten into a firestorm of flying bullets with a handful of dangerous gangbangers.

However, nothing he'd ever experienced before in his life had made him as nervous as he now was as he faced a woman with soft curls and green eyes and a spirit that made him smile.

"You've been terribly quiet all day," he observed.

She nodded. "I guess I've just been trying to figure out where we go from here."

"I know where I'd like us to go from here." He set his coffee cup on the table and ignored the sudden dryness of his throat as he held her gaze intently.

"Where is that?" she asked. She picked up her coffee cup and took a sip.

"Jordon, I'm not talking about these cases. I'm talking about us...you and me."

Her eyes became guarded as she set her cup back on the nightstand. "Gabriel, there is no you and me."

"Jordon, I'm in love with you and I think you feel the same way about me." His heart thundered in his chest as he spoke the words that had been burning inside him.

She averted her gaze from his. "You just feel that way because we slept together."

"Jordon, I loved making love with you, but

my feelings for you certainly aren't just based on a physical level. I love the way your eyes light up just before you say something funny. I adore how they narrow when you're deep in thought."

He leaned forward, the words now falling out of his mouth as if released from a pressure cooker. "Jordon, at the end of this, no matter how the investigation goes, I don't want to tell you goodbye. I want you in my life forever. I want…" He paused as she held up her hand.

"Stop, Gabriel. Please stop." She got up from the edge of the bed and walked several steps back from where he sat.

He drew in a deep breath and then continued. "I know the distance thing might be a bit of an issue at first, but it's less than a four-hour drive from here to Kansas City. There's no reason why we couldn't continue to see each other on days off and eventually I'd be willing to relocate."

There was no joy on her beautiful features. Instead she gazed at him in what looked like stunned horror. She closed her eyes for a brief moment, and when she opened them again, a reckless smile curved her lips. "Sorry, sailor. You've obviously got me mixed up with somebody else."

"Stop it, Jordon." He stood, all of his muscles tense. "Don't make jokes when I'm pouring out my heart to you."

A slight flush filled her cheeks and she averted her gaze from him. "Then stop pouring out your heart," she replied in a soft voice.

"Okay, I'll shut up after you tell me you don't love me." He took several steps closer to her. "Tell me that I mean nothing to you and I'll leave here and won't speak of this again."

He saw it in her eyes, a soft yearning, a sweet wistfulness, but it was there only a moment and then her chin shot up and her gaze was once again shuttered.

"I told you I wasn't marriage material, that I'd never lived up to anyone's expectations," she replied.

"Oh, Jordon, you've not only lived up to mine, but you've far exceeded them," he said softly.

Her lower lip began to tremble and she turned away from him. "Please go, Gabriel. Before you say anything more that you'll regret."

He stared at her stiff back and he didn't see an impenetrable wall. Rather, he saw a woman who was afraid to believe she was worthy of being loved by anyone.

He didn't know how to make her not be

afraid. He didn't know what else to say and so he simply stood still and loved her.

JORDON WAITED FOR the sound of the door opening and then closing, indicating to her that Gabriel had left. But several long minutes passed and it didn't happen.

Her heart hurt as it had never ached before in her life.

Falling in love with Gabriel had been so incredibly easy, but this…this rejection of him was so achingly difficult. She desperately wanted what he was offering her, yet of all the men in the entire world she knew, she couldn't be more wrong for a man like him.

She stiffened as his hands fell on her shoulders. "Jordon," he whispered, his breath a warm delight on her ear. She closed her eyes and fought against the sting of tears. "Jordon, don't throw away what we have."

She drew in a deep breath and whirled back around to face him, dislodging his hands from her. "You obviously took things too seriously. We don't have anything, Gabriel. We slept together. It was no big deal. We've had a few laughs and some good times, but that certainly doesn't equate love."

He stared at her and the intensity of his gaze made her feel as if he was peering into her mind, into the very depths of her soul. "What are you so afraid of?"

"I'm not afraid of anything," she replied with a rise of anger filling her. Why was he making this so difficult? Why couldn't he just accept the words she said and go away?

"You know what I think? I believe your parents and your ex-husband did a real number on your head. They have made you feel like you're unworthy of loving...of being loved, and nothing could be further from the truth."

"Thank you, Dr. Gabriel, for the quick psychoanalysis," she retorted.

He had the audacity to smile at her. "You have no idea how adorable, how utterly wonderful I find you. I've been waiting years to find you. You're the woman I want to build a life with. I want you to have my children and I want to grow old with you."

His words painted a picture of a beautiful future, one that she'd once dreamed of and one that still resonated with desire in a small piece of her heart.

There was a part of her that wanted to reach out and grasp on to what he offered, but there was a bigger voice inside her head that told her she'd be all kinds of fool to believe that kind of future with him could be hers.

"You're just trying to grasp on to something good because your investigation has stalled out and you're frustrated," she replied.

A flash of anger lit the depths of his eyes. "You really believe my feelings for you are simply born out of my frustration with the investigation?" He released a dry laugh and shook his head. "Don't try to tell me how I feel and why. I'm not afraid to take a leap of faith with you."

"Then you're a fool," she exclaimed. "And stop implying that I'm afraid. I'm a realist, Gabriel, not a coward."

"I think you're a coward," he replied. "I think you love me, Jordon, and you're just too scared to give us a chance. You'll invite a serial killer into your life, but you won't allow in a man who loves you. You're more afraid of giving your heart than you are in giving your life."

"Get out." A deep rich anger filled her. "Get out now." She stalked to the door. She didn't want to hear anything else he felt the need to say to her.

He stood perfectly still, the only movement his gaze as it searched her features. He finally walked over to the chair, grabbed his coat and put it on.

She opened the door, allowing in the cold

of the night, a cold that couldn't begin to compete with the chill that encased her heart.

He walked over to her and reached up as if to stroke her cheek, but she jerked away from him, not allowing him the touch. A muscle ticked in his jaw and his eyes darkened.

"You aren't just a coward, Jordon. You're also a beautiful fool," he said and then walked out.

She slammed the door after him. She locked it and then leaned with her back against it as tears blurred her vision. A beautiful fool...a coward. How dare he say such things to her.

Who did he think he was? He didn't really know her and he certainly couldn't be in love with her. He was just kidding himself and she refused to be pulled into his fantasy.

Still, her heart squeezed tight, so tight in her chest she could scarcely draw a breath. He was the fool to think that she could be the woman he wanted in his life.

She moved away from the door and sank down on the bed, tears still stinging her eyes and an imminent threat of sobs only making her even angrier with him.

He was just a silly man who had confused a wonderful bout of lovemaking and a few laughs with love. She'd told him right up front how she felt about marriage and relationships. He should have just kept his feelings to himself.

But what if he does really love you, a little voice whispered in her head. *What if fate brought you together to finally know happiness? To finally have what you've always dreamed of in the deepest recesses of your heart?*

"No," she said aloud, effectively silencing the voice in her head. She wasn't a coward, but she just wasn't willing to put her heart on the line again.

She'd be gone from here before long and eventually Gabriel would find the woman who was really right for him. She'd be a woman who had a place for everything and everything in its place. She'd be able to cook hearty meals for him and whatever children they might have. She'd be everything Jordon wasn't and couldn't be.

Damn him for his bedroom eyes and gentle ways. Damn him for making her love him when she didn't want to love anyone. Tears began to chase themselves down her cheeks, and instead of attempting to stanch them, she gave in to them.

She curled up on the bed and wept. She grieved for the woman she had once been, a young woman who had believed in dreams of marriage and happily-ever-after.

She mourned the fact that she no longer believed in those dreams, that they had been shattered by a man who had taken her love and then betrayed it over and over again.

It felt as if she cried for hours, and finally, her tears wound down to little gasping sobs. She rolled over on her back and stared up at the ceiling. How was she going to continue working with Gabriel when she was so angry with him?

And why are you so angry?

The reason wasn't clear, but she embraced the emotion and held tight to it. She was a lone wolf and he should respect that. The idea that he thought she could be anything else just ticked her off.

She got up from the bed and went into the bathroom, where she sluiced water over her face and then stared at her reflection in the mirror.

Finish this assignment and then get the heck out of Dodge, she mentally said to her reflection. *Do your time and then get back to the safe, alone life you've built for yourself.*

Eventually she'd forget that she'd ever loved a good man like Gabriel. She had to forget him because there was no place in her life for him.

She left the bathroom and started to unbuckle her holster, but stopped as she spied a piece of paper peeking out from under her door. Her heartbeat clanged a discordant beat as she pulled her gun. She raced to the door, unlocked it and yanked it open. The porch was empty and she narrowed her eyes to attempt to see through the darkness.

She remained standing on alert for several long moments, the night feeling ominous and fraught with new danger. Slowly she bent down, picked up the paper and then closed and locked her door.

The white paper burned in her hand as she carried it with her and perched on the edge of the bed. When had it been shoved under her door?

It had to have been left after Gabriel had gone, otherwise he would have seen it. While she'd been crying about broken dreams and Gabriel's love, the killer had left her a new calling card.

Her hands trembled as she opened the paper and read the bold letters.

Play a game of cat and mouse
In Mouse's Maze of Mirrors

Come alone or I won't play
At midnight face your fears.

She read the note a second time and then looked at the clock on the nightstand. It was twenty till midnight.

She jumped up off the bed and pulled her cell phone from her pocket. *Come alone or I won't play.* The words reverberated in her head.

This was a final showdown. She knew it in her gut. With her hand still trembling and a healthy fear squeezing her lungs, she repocketed her cell phone.

She threw on her coat and then grabbed the keys to the patrol car that she hadn't used since she'd been here. She left the room and headed for the parking lot.

She was a lone wolf, and she was going to meet the killer in a place where her nightmares began.

Chapter Thirteen

Who was she going to face in the mirrors? Jordon clenched the steering wheel tight as she drove through the dark night toward the tourist attraction.

Would it be Kevin Rollings, who worked the admission gate and probably knew every inch of the maze? Was he the one they sought?

Or would it be one of his brothers? Was Ed not the pleasant handyman he pretended to be? Had Glen managed to lose his tail? Had he parked his car at his home and then sneaked out of a door or window to come here for a final confrontation with her?

A simmering panic rose up the back of her throat and she swallowed hard against it. Would she get into the maze and get lost in her past? Captured and helpless by visions of Ralph Hicks and that cellar where she'd thought she would die?

She couldn't let that happen, otherwise whoever was in the maze would manage to accomplish what Ralph hadn't managed. If she gave in to her panic, then she knew without a doubt she would wind up dead.

It was three minutes until midnight when she pulled into the Mouse's Maze of Mirrors parking lot. There were no other cars in the lot and the place was dark and formidable.

She got out of the car with her gun in her hand, every muscle tensed and her heart racing a familiar rhythm of fear. Would he be here? Or was this just another little game of taunting like the missing bell in the guest shed?

She wouldn't know until she went inside. She licked her dry lips and drew on every ounce of training she'd had. She had to remain cool and calm and completely in control.

The front door was unlocked, an invitation to enter and face the killer. She eased the door open and went inside in a crouched position. Security lights gave the small lobby a ghostly illumination.

She checked behind the counter where Kevin had sat when she and Gabriel had been there before. Her lungs expelled a deep breath as she saw that nobody was there.

She stared at the turnstile, knowing that once she went through it she would be in the maze of mirrors. *You can do this*, she told herself. *You're a kick-butt FBI agent and it's time to put an end to the killer's madness.*

Her stomach twisted in knots so tight she was half-nauseous. Her lungs constricted, making deep breaths impossible. *Just do it*, a voice screamed in her head.

She pushed through the turnstile and stepped into the maze. Lights turned on and five reflections of herself stared back at her. She appeared wild-eyed and terrified...just like she'd appeared in Ralph's mirrors.

She drew in several deep breaths to center herself. She refused to be that frightened woman in the reflection. She didn't move until she'd calmed herself and was prepared for whatever might happen.

"Hello?" she called out.

Silence.

Was she here all alone or did she share the space with the person who had brutally killed three people? Somebody had to have turned on the lights. She couldn't be alone. After taking several steps to her right, she found herself facing another set of mirrors.

Which way had Gabriel led her out of here? She couldn't remember how to find the exit, and in any case, she expected to meet somebody before she ever reached the end of the maze. "Is anybody here?"

"Beware. If you aren't fast enough, I'll pull you into my mouse hole and nobody will ever find you again."

The words boomed overhead and ended on the mouse's cackle. Jordon whirled around and five Jordons moved in the reflections. Her taut nerves ached as she waited for somebody to show themselves.

Was she supposed to wait for someone to appear or walk the maze to meet her tormentor at another junction? The uncertainty of the situation had her silently screaming inside her head.

She took several steps forward only to realize it was a mirror and not a passageway. She walked to the left and found another corridor.

A flash of movement behind her spun her around, but then she realized it had been a reflection and she had no idea where the person was and how close he was to her.

The vision had been so brief there was no way she could make an identification. She didn't even know if it had been a man or a woman. It only confirmed to her that the killer was here and toying with her.

She walked slowly, the panic still attempting to close off her airway as she faced her own reflection again and again. The odor of cigarette smoke seemed to linger in the air, along with the acrid scent of burning flesh.

The scars on her hip burned and itched, a reminder of her nightmares, of Ralph and his torture. *Be in the moment*, she commanded herself. She couldn't be pulled back to that cellar where she'd thought she was going to die a slow and painful death.

"Bring it on, you little creep," she yelled.

A girlish giggle filled the air. "You're gonna die in here tonight, Agent James."

Jordon froze, her mind working to make sense of the familiar voice. It couldn't be... Hannah? Was this some sort of a teenager's sick joke? Was she here with some of her friends? Spooking the FBI agent? Was this their idea of a little fun?

"Hannah? Stop playing. This isn't funny. Stop this nonsense and come out and talk to me right now," she said.

"I don't want to talk. You're the next victim, Jordon. You're staying at Diamond Cove and that means you have to die."

Jordon's skin crawled. Was it possible? Surely the murders couldn't have been committed by a fifteen-year-old girl. But even as she tried to deny the possibility, she knew the facts, and the fact was even teenagers could be deadly killers.

Something flashed in her peripheral vision on her left and pain sliced into her upper arm. She whirled around, but Hannah was gone, once again hidden within the maze. Her breath caught in her throat as the warmth of blood leaking down her arm attested to the depth of the wound.

This was definitely no joke. This wasn't a silly game, not when blood had been drawn. Her brain whirled. None of the murdered guests would have felt threatened by Hannah. Hannah knew the woods and she would have known the guests' routines. She had the means to commit the murders, but more than anything Jordon needed to understand the motive.

"Why, Hannah? Why are you doing this? Why did you kill those people?"

"Because I want to go home!" Hannah's voice was filled with a bitter rage. "I didn't want to move to this stupid place in the first place. I don't belong here. Now nobody will want to stay at Diamond Cove and my mom and dad will take us back to Oklahoma City, where I have my own friends."

Jordon was stunned, first by the vitriol in Hannah's voice and second by the unbelievable cunning that had hatched this whole deadly plot.

She tightened her grip on her gun and a vision of Joan's face flashed in her mind. Joan, with her sweet blue eyes and her love for her family—there wasn't going to be a happy ending for her.

But could Jordon shoot Joan's daughter? Could she really take the life of a fifteen-year-old girl? Hopefully, it wouldn't come to that, but if it came to which one of them was going to walk out of here alive, Jordon would pull her trigger without regret.

She screamed as a knife sliced out at her from the left, catching her in the middle of her thigh. She pivoted and ran to the left and caught a glimpse of Hannah ahead of her.

"Stop! Hannah, don't make me shoot you!"

Hannah laughed and instantly disappeared from Jordon's view. Jordon stopped her forward run and instead crept forward slowly… cautiously, unsure from where the next attack might come.

Her biggest fear was that the attack would come from behind. That she wouldn't see Hannah coming, she wouldn't hear her approach until a knife plunged into the center of her back.

There was no question the surroundings

were disorienting for Jordon, and it was equally obvious Hannah was perfectly at home in the maze. Like the mouse that ruled this environment, Hannah was the rodent that knew all the secrets of the mirrors.

The sticky wetness on her arm and the blood that now had soaked through her slacks concerned her, but she couldn't focus on that now. She had to figure out a way to somehow disarm and contain Hannah without either of them getting killed.

GABRIEL DROVE AIMLESSLY in his car, the argument with Jordon playing and replaying in his head and sickening his heart. He'd been a damned fool to tell her how he felt about her.

He should have at least waited until the day before she was leaving. Maybe with another week of spending more time together she would have been more open to the possibility of a continuing relationship.

She obviously hadn't been ready to hear what he had to say. Maybe his timing sucked, but he didn't believe she didn't care about him. He'd seen love or something very much like it shining in her eyes when she gazed at him in quiet moments of their days. He'd felt it wafting from her when they touched and when they laughed.

What he hated was that they'd parted with harsh words. While he believed what he'd said to her about being afraid to reach out for love, he'd probably been too harsh with her. He'd let his emotions get ahead of him.

He hated that her cold, demanding parents and a cheating ex-husband had made her believe that she was unlovable. He hated that she didn't believe she deserved to be loved.

He found himself parked back in the Diamond Cove parking lot and realized he was here to apologize to her. He'd pushed her too hard and he didn't want to go to bed until he told her he was sorry.

A glance at the clock told him it was a few minutes before midnight. It was possible she was already sleeping. He could always apologize to her in the morning. Still, he didn't turn around and leave.

Just as he'd needed to tell her how he felt about her earlier, he knew he needed to apologize to her this very moment. The cold air gripped him as he got out of his car. The same cold had encased his heart since he'd left her room earlier.

He certainly didn't intend to apologize for loving her, but he wanted her to know he hadn't meant to get upset with her and that he just wanted her to be happy. At least that way hopefully there would be no unresolved tension between them in the morning.

The last week with her shouldn't be uncomfortable for them both. That wasn't the impression he wanted her to take away from here.

As he approached her door, he was relieved to see light casting out from her window. Good—apparently she was still awake.

He rapped lightly on the door and waited for a reply. When none came he knocked a little harder. "Jordon, it's me. I'd like to talk to you. Please open the door."

Several seconds passed and a rivulet of uneasiness swept through him. There was no way he believed her to be the kind of woman to just ignore him. He knew her well enough to know that if she was still angry with him she'd open her door and meet him with both barrels loaded.

He froze. Had the patrol car he'd left for her to use while here been in the parking lot? He'd been so buried in his own head, so deep in his own thoughts, he hadn't paid any attention.

He turned and raced back to the parking lot. The uneasiness turned to panic as he saw the car was missing. Where could she have gone? Why would she leave her room at this time of night?

Would she have been angry enough to get in the car and go for a drive? That just didn't feel right. For several long seconds his brain refused to fire.

Had something happened after he'd left her earlier? What could have possibly led her to leave her room at this time of night?

Had the killer made contact with her again?

He stared across the street where the Overton house was dark. He needed to get into Jordon's room. He had to see if there was any clue inside as to her whereabouts. Maybe she just needed to get out and clear her head, he thought again as he raced across the street. Maybe she got hungry and decided to grab something to eat.

However, in winter in Branson on a weeknight, most places shut down early. Besides, he just didn't believe one of those rational explanations was right.

Although he hated to bother the Overton family, an alarm bell was ringing loudly in his head, an alarm that told him Jordon might just be in trouble.

He pushed the doorbell and heard the dingdong echo someplace inside the house. He waited only a minute and then rang it again.

Lights went on inside and Ted came to the door clad in a T-shirt and plaid sleep pants and holding a gun.

"Chief Walters," he said in surprise.

"I need you to open Jordon's door for me," Gabriel said without preamble.

"Give me a minute." He opened the door to allow Gabriel to step into a small entry and then Ted disappeared down a hallway. He returned a few moments later wearing his coat and jeans and they both left the house.

"Is there a problem?" Ted asked.

"I'm not sure." Gabriel's gut twisted into knots of tension. He'd half hoped that by the time they got back to her suite she'd have pulled in, sheepish that she'd worried anyone and carrying a bag of goodies from the nearest all-night convenience store.

"I hope I didn't wake everyone in your house," he said.

"Just me and Joan. It would take a bomb going off to wake up Jason or Hannah at this time of the night," Ted replied.

When they reached her room, Ted pulled from his pocket a ring full of keys. He fumbled with them for a moment and then got to the one that would unlock her door.

Gabriel stepped into the room and gazed around, his heart beating wildly. Almost immediately he saw the white folded piece of paper on her bed.

His chest tightened. It looked just like the previous note she'd received from the killer. He picked it up and opened it. His blood chilled as he read the sick poem.

"I've got to go," he said to Ted. "Don't touch anything in here. Just lock up after me."

He didn't wait for Ted to reply. He ran out of the room and down the path to his car, his heartbeat thundering loudly in his head. He had to find her. Dear God, he had to get to her as soon as possible.

When he got into his car, he looked at the time. Twenty after midnight. She'd met the killer twenty minutes ago in a place where she'd frozen in a panic attack when they'd been there before.

She would not only be vulnerable to a bloodthirsty, knife-wielding killer, but also to the horrible demons of her past. Why hadn't she called him the minute she'd received the note?

Even as the question formed in his mind, he knew the answer. She'd been so angry with him and the note had said for her to come alone. Dammit!

He tore out of the parking lot and tried to call her, but the call went directly to her voice mail. What was happening? He glanced at the clock. What had already happened? It had been almost half an hour since the rendezvous was supposed to occur. So many horrible things could transpire in that amount of time.

He tried to call her again and got the same result. He then called Ben Hammond. The private investigator answered on the second ring.

"You have men on Glen and Kevin Rollings?"

"Yeah. When my guys last checked in they were both at their homes."

"Have them knock on the doors and get a visual confirmation that those two are where they're supposed to be and then get back to me as soon as possible," Gabriel said urgently.

Ben called back just as Gabriel turned into the Mouse's Maze of Mirrors parking lot, where Jordon's car was the only other vehicle in the lot.

"Both men are confirmed at their homes," Ben said. "My men spoke to each of them."

"Thanks, Ben."

Gabriel pulled his car to a stop, his brain whirling with not just fear, but complete confusion. If Ted was at home, and Kevin and

Glen Rollings were also in their houses, then who the hell was inside with Jordon?

"HANNAH, COME OUT and talk to me," Jordon shouted. For the last few minutes the girl had been ominously silent. Jordon had no idea where she was in the maze now or how to find her to end the madness.

She'd wandered down corridors, wound up in dead ends, and all the while her nerves had screamed with tension as she anticipated another attack.

She thought the bleeding of her wounds had finally stopped, but the anxiety of the situation was definitely wearing on her. She had no idea how much time had passed since she'd first entered the maze but it felt like an eternity.

The recorded cackle of the mouse split the air and Jordon dropped into a crouch, prepared for an attack that might come from any direction.

Her own reflections haunted her. Her mind attempted to drag her back into the torment of her past. There were times she saw only herself and other times she saw the ghost of Ralph Hicks just behind her. She wanted to scream with the anxiety that bubbled inside her.

"Hannah, this needs to stop now."

"You're right."

The girl's voice came from all around her and a sharp pain in the back stole Jordon's breath away. She jerked around to see Hannah's reflection in four mirrors. The girl smiled and held up her bloody knife.

Jordon's knees tried to buckle as she took a step forward and the warmth of blood worked down her spine. Her gun hand shook as she stared at the four Hannahs.

Which one was real?

Time seemed to stand still and then everything happened in the space of a single heartbeat. Jordon fired at one Hannah. Glass shattered to the floor. Damn, she'd shot a mirror.

She gasped in agonizing pain and tears blurred her vision. If she had to shoot out every mirror in the place, she'd do it. She scarcely took time to breathe before she fired again, and this time her bullet found its mark.

Hannah screamed and dropped her knife as she bent over to grab just above her left knee. She took a step forward and then fell out of the reflections and to the floor.

It was over.

Case solved.

Jordon tucked her gun into her holster, the

simple action taking up nearly all of her energy as her chest squeezed tight and her back screamed in pain.

She walked over close enough to kick the knife out of Hannah's reach and then took several steps backward. She was so tired…so very tired as the adrenaline that had pumped through her for so long seeped away.

She'd just sit for a minute to catch her breath and then she'd call Gabriel. She sank down and leaned back. She was light-headed and cold chills raced through her.

Hannah continued to yell and curse and cry, but the sound seemed to come from very far away. Jordon saw herself in three reflections and she was vaguely surprised that no visions from her past haunted her, no images of Ralph Hicks and that cellar tried to intrude. She saw only herself, alone as she had always been.

The pain in her back intensified, making it difficult to breathe. She wondered if she might be dying. The thought made her so sad.

She should have called Gabriel. Her heart squeezed tight at thoughts of him. He'd have to clean up this mess she'd made. At least Hannah would no longer be able to hurt anyone again.

White dots like snowflakes danced in her

vision. Cold. She was so very cold. She was back in a snow globe, immersed in a brutal, bitter winter.

She closed her eyes.

She should have gone home and danced in her underwear.

Chapter Fourteen

Gabriel approached the front door of the maze with his heart beating out of his chest. He had no idea what to expect or who besides Jordon he might encounter inside.

Billy Bond was in jail and all their other suspects were accounted for, so whoever had written that note hadn't even been on their radar. Who could it be?

He went into the front door fast and with his gun ready. The small lobby was empty. He shoved through the turnstile and entered the maze. Instantly he heard female cries for help coming from someplace within the mirrors.

His nerves electrified. Was it Jordon? No... he didn't think so. Whoever it was, she was not only cursing but she was also crying for her mother.

Definitely not Jordon.

His mouth dried. So, where was Jordon?

The unknowns of the situation balled a huge knot of anxiety in his stomach. He should call for backup, but until he knew what he faced, he was afraid that the extra manpower might only complicate things.

He stood in a corridor where he saw nothing but visions of himself. He walked forward and took the first turn to the right. Another empty passageway.

The cries for help had stopped and a frightening silence ensued. A horrible dread seeped into his bones as he continued walking slowly, aware that somebody could jump out and attack him with every step he took.

Had the cries for help been a ploy? A ruse to get him to rush to the rescue only to be stabbed by the killer? Was that what had happened to Jordon?

Oh, God—please, no. She might not want to have a meaningful relationship with him, but he certainly wanted her alive and well and with a future that would hopefully bring her to the point where she could love some special man. He didn't want her hurt. He prayed she wasn't hurt.

Walking the maze was agonizingly slow as he constantly turned first one way and then the other to clear any corridors he came to.

He finally stopped with his back to a dead

end. "Jordon!" Her name released from the very depths of him with more than a hint of despair. "Jordon, where are you?"

"I'm here. Please help me. I'm hurt." The female voice came from his left and he suddenly recognized it.

"Hannah?" he called out incredulously. What on earth was she doing in here?

"She shot me. I just came here to help her and she accidentally shot me," Hannah cried.

"Where's Jordon?" Gabriel tried to move in the direction of the voice.

"She's here. She's…she's dead. He stabbed her and then he ran away."

Gabriel stumbled into one of the mirrors as all the breath in his body whooshed out of him. *No!* The single word screamed in his brain. It couldn't be. An all-encompassing grief pierced through him as he shoved off the mirror and continued walking.

He couldn't think about Jordon right now. He had to shove the grief away. He needed to focus. He pulled his radio from his belt and called in the troops.

From what little he knew, this was definitely a crime scene and the killer was still on the loose. With the call made, he reattached the radio to his belt.

"Hannah, keep talking so I can find you."

He pulled on every ounce of professionalism he had. Jordon was gone. Jordon was dead. Despite the utter tearing of his heart, he had a job to do.

Hannah continued to yell to him, and with two more turns, he was there. His brain worked to take in the scene before him. Hannah lay on the floor, bleeding from what appeared to be a gunshot wound in her leg. A bloody knife was also on the floor not too far away.

It was the sight of Jordon that once again stole his breath away and squeezed his lungs so hard he could scarcely breathe. She was seated and leaning against one of the mirrors, eyes closed and utterly lifeless.

He rushed to her side and crouched down, his fingers going to her neck to check for a pulse. *Please be there*, he prayed. *Please don't be dead.*

Yes! Yes, there was a pulse.

He grabbed his radio once again. "I need an ambulance at Mouse's Maze of Mirrors. Officer down. I repeat, officer down!" He touched her face. Her skin was cold and pale.

"Jordon? Jordon, can you open your eyes? Can you talk to me?" There was no response.

Her slacks were ripped and bloody across her thigh, but it appeared that the wound had stopped bleeding. He had no idea what other injuries she might have sustained.

He was afraid to move her to even check. Hannah had said she'd been stabbed by the killer. More injuries had to be in her back or someplace where he couldn't see them beneath her coat.

"What about me? I'm hurt. She shot me," Hannah cried plaintively.

Reluctantly, he left Jordon's side and moved to Hannah. The bullet had caught her just above her knee, and while she was bleeding, it was apparent that nothing vital had been hit because there wasn't too much blood.

"Just hang on," he said to the girl. "Help is on its way."

"Is Agent James going to be all right?" Hannah asked and there was a glint of fear in her dark eyes.

Gabriel took a step back and surveyed the scene once again. Hannah shot and Jordon apparently stabbed and the knife was on scene.

There was no way the killer would have left his weapon behind. It didn't make sense and the murderer they'd been chasing didn't make those kinds of mistakes. There was no way he could believe things had happened as Hannah had said.

A new quiet horror swept through him as

he looked back at her. Was it possible that the tall, slender girl was responsible for all the deaths and destruction?

"It's over, Hannah," he said in calculation. "Agent James is going to be just fine and she'll be able to tell me everything that happened here tonight." He wanted to believe it. He needed to believe that Jordon would be okay.

Hannah's features twisted with rage. "I just wanted to go home! If nobody stayed at Diamond Cove because of the murders then Mom and Dad would move back to Oklahoma City and I'd be where I belong."

"Chief Walters," a deep voice cried out. "We're here."

Gabriel recognized the voice as belonging to Ty Kincaid, an EMT. "We need two boards," Gabriel replied.

It seemed to take forever for the medical team to find them in the maze and then get both Hannah and Jordon loaded into the ambulance.

Jordon didn't regain consciousness as they took off her coat to reveal the bloody wound on her back. Gabriel officially placed Hannah under arrest before the ambulance pulled away.

He followed the ambulance to the hospital,

where both patients were whisked back into the emergency room and he was left alone in the lobby.

Gabriel paced the room, his thoughts a riotous mess in his head. Hannah was their killer. How deep were Jordon's wounds? A fifteen-year-old kid had kept them all hopping around like maniacs all because she didn't want to live here. Had he gotten there in time or had Jordon been stabbed deep enough in her back to cause her death?

Only now did he fully process the sheer anguish that ripped through him, bringing the sting of tears to his eyes and squeezing his heart with an agony he'd never known before.

He was ragged with emotions by the time Mark walked in to join him in his vigil. "How is she?" he asked.

"Nobody has told me anything yet." He sank down on a chair and Mark sat next to him.

"She's a fighter," Mark replied.

"She is that," Gabriel agreed, but that didn't stop the frantic claw of despair inside him.

"The men were all working at the crime scene when I left them. I contacted Kent Myers to let him know he'd have to keep the attraction closed until we're finished with it."

"At least it's over now except the evidence

gathering and the cleanup," Gabriel replied as he stared at the emergency room door and willed a doctor to come out with good news.

"Who would have thought our perp would turn out to be a teenage girl? You think the prosecutor will push to try her as an adult?"

Gabriel turned to look at Mark. "I'm certainly going to encourage him to. These murders weren't the result of a school yard fight or something else spontaneous. She carefully plotted this out. She showed enormous cunning in both the planning and the execution. She needs to be locked up for a very long time."

He turned to stare at the door once again. What was taking so long? Why didn't somebody come out to talk to him?

"Want some coffee?" Mark asked.

"No, thanks. I'm good." As sick as his stomach was at the moment, there was no way he wanted to attempt drinking anything.

Dr. Gordon Oakley came through the emergency room door. Gabriel and Mark both sprang to their feet. "Chief… Mark," he greeted them.

Gabriel searched the ER doctor's features. "How is she?"

"Agent James is resting easy now. She needed seven stitches in her leg and twenty-one in her back. Thankfully, both were slashing wounds and not stabbing injuries. She was also cut on her arm, but that didn't require any stitches."

Gabriel released a deep sigh of relief and then frowned. "So, why was she unconscious?"

"I'd say she might have suffered a touch of shock and utter exhaustion. She's hooked up to an IV. We've cleaned her up and administered pain meds. We'll keep her under observation until sometime tomorrow."

"Can I see her?"

"I'd prefer that she not be disturbed for the rest of the night. From what I understand, she's been through quite a trauma and what she needs now is complete rest," Gordon replied. "You can see her in the morning."

Although disappointed, Gabriel nodded. He wanted whatever was best for her. For the next ten minutes the doctor filled them in on Hannah's wound. At the moment she was in surgery. Her parents had been contacted and were in a private waiting room.

"I'll go talk to the Overtons," Mark said when the doctor had left them again.

"And I want a full-time guard on Hannah while she recuperates here," Gabriel replied. "I need to get back to the crime scene."

"I'll take care of everything here," Mark assured him.

The two men parted, as Mark headed to talk to the Overtons and Gabriel left the building. It wasn't until he was in his car that the emotions of the night nearly overwhelmed him.

As his car warmed up, he leaned his head back and closed his eyes. She was going to be just fine. Tears of relief burned at his eyes.

He'd been so scared for her. He'd been so afraid that this night would end differently. It was already tragic enough that a girl's life, for all intents and purposes, had come to an end.

It was utterly inconceivable that three innocent people had been brutally murdered because a kid didn't like where she was living. But if Jordon had lost her life tonight, the depth of the tragedy would have been beyond anything he could even imagine.

She was fine. The case was solved, and within the next twenty-four to forty-eight hours, she would be gone from here, gone forever from his life.

He tightened his hands on the steering wheel, opened his eyes and realized it had begun to snow.

JORDON AWOKE SLOWLY. Before she opened her eyes the scent of fresh coffee and bacon drifted to her nose along with a faint antiseptic smell. Shoes squeaked on the floor from someplace in the distance and a blood-pressure cuff began to pump up on her arm.

She opened her eyes to find herself alone in a hospital room. The cuff around her arm released and the blood-pressure monitor displayed numbers that assured her she'd made it through the long night despite the aches and pains that attempted to tell her otherwise.

She glanced out the nearby window and frowned. It was snowing again. She couldn't wait to get to that beach in Florida, where it would be wonderfully warm and sunny.

"Ah, good—you're awake." A blonde woman in purple scrubs entered her room. "My name is Marjorie and I'll be your nurse for the day." She walked over to Jordon and held out a thermometer. "Open."

Jordon did as she was told.

"You're normal," Marjorie replied as she removed the thermometer.

"I know some people who would argue with you about that," Jordon replied and then frowned as Marjorie didn't react. Great—a nurse without a sense of humor.

"On a scale from one to ten, how do you rate your pain level?"

Jordon changed positions and winced. "About a seven, but I don't need any more pain meds." She almost welcomed the pain that was a reminder that she'd survived. "What I would like is a big cup of coffee."

"I'll contact the kitchen and let them know you're ready for a breakfast tray."

"Perfect," Jordon replied.

She stared back out the window as Marjorie left the room. Gabriel. A vision of him jumped into her head. So handsome and with those piercing blue eyes that warmed her from the inside out.

She channeled her thoughts into another direction. She didn't want to think of him with his gentle touches and strength of character.

Instead she closed her eyes and thought about Hannah and the confrontation from the night before. She'd been a fool to go in there alone, especially not knowing whom she might face.

It had been a reckless move not to call for backup. She wasn't a cat with nine lives. She'd already had two near-death experiences because of her lone-wolf attitude. It was past time to be a team player.

Thankfully, these troubling thoughts were interrupted by the arrival of breakfast. As she ate she was haunted by every breakfast she had shared with the Overtons, by each conversation she'd had with Joan.

Hannah's crimes would haunt them. Their lives would never be the same again. How did a parent ever find any kind of peace knowing that one of their children had committed three horrible murders? That she would be in lockup for years to come?

She cleaned off her plate and then fell back asleep. She had no nightmares haunted by Ralph Hicks or Hannah. Rather it was Gabriel who filled her dreams. They were sweet dreams of laughter and love, and she awakened with both deep longing and agonizing regret.

By that time lunch was served and then the doctor arrived. "When can I get out of here?" she asked him.

"How are you feeling? We did a lot of stitching on you last night."

"I'm sore," she admitted. "But I'm hoping to get a ride out of here as soon as possible and get back home to Kansas City. I can see my doctor there for any follow-up."

"Why don't you enjoy dinner on us this evening and then we'll see about releasing you," he replied.

She nodded her agreement, but there was no way she was spending another night here. She needed to get home. She had to get her feet back on the ground in her own space and put this place and a certain man far behind her.

After the doctor left the room, she called Director Tom Langford to fill him in on everything that had happened. He arranged for a helicopter to pick her up the next afternoon.

She'd just hung up when Gabriel came in. She stared at him in stunned surprise. In one arm he carried a huge, inflatable palm tree and in the other he had a pink fruity drink with a little umbrella stirrer.

"If Jordon can't get to Florida, then a piece of Florida will come to her," he said. He set the palm tree next to her bed. "Unfortunately, there's no alcohol in here." He held out the drink.

She took it from him and fought against the huge lump in her throat that made speech impossible for a moment. He looked so wonderfully handsome in his uniform and without the stress of the cases weighing him down.

He sat in the chair next to her bed and smiled at her. "Go on—take a sip. I wasn't sure exactly what you liked, so it's a strawberry smoothie with chunks of pineapple, berries and mango."

She took a drink and she didn't know if it tasted so good because she loved smoothies or if it was the fact that he'd gone to all this trouble just for her. The silly man was breaking her heart.

"Delicious," she said and then pointed to the palm tree. "Where did you manage to get that?"

"A couple of years ago the police department threw themselves a luau. There are five more of those in storage." His smile faded. "How are you doing?"

"I'm okay. I guess I'll be sporting a new scar across my back."

"She could have killed you." His voice was husky and his beautiful eyes were dark and filled with an emotion she didn't want to acknowledge.

"Is this the part where you yell at me for being a reckless fool?"

He leaned back in the chair. "It's enough for me that you recognize that you were reckless."

"I should have called you the minute I got that note. I'm done being a cowboy. I got lucky when Ralph Hicks had me in that cellar. I got lucky again last night, but I can't depend on luck anymore."

"If you've realized that then I guess your time here wasn't for nothing." His gaze on her was so intense she had to look away.

"How is Hannah?"

She needed a conversation about something…anything that would ease some of the tension in the room.

She stared out the window and listened absently as he caught her up on everything that was going on with the teenage killer. Hannah had come through surgery fine and was recuperating with a guard at her door.

"We found Joan's car parked a block away from the maze. She sneaked out of the house and took the car. Ted and Joan heard nothing. Hannah intended to kill you and then get home and back into bed before morning," he said.

"How are Ted and Joan?"

"Broken and in complete shock."

"They'll eventually get through this," Jordon replied. "They're strong people." She cast her gaze out the window. "And now, on another note, I should be released sometime this evening and I've made arrangements to leave tomorrow. I was wondering if you could pick me up later and take me to a motel for the night," she said.

She looked at him once again and saw in his eyes words he wanted to speak, emotions he wanted to share. But she didn't want to hear him. They had said everything necessary the night before.

"You know I'll be here whenever you need me," he finally replied.

Once again the lump was back in her throat and the pain that had been in her back moved around to pierce her in the heart.

"I'll call you later," she said and set the drink on her tray. "I think what I need right now is a nap."

He got up from the chair. "Then I'll just wait for your call." With those words he was gone.

She squeezed her eyes closed against a sudden burn of unexpected tears. The whole visit had been stilted and uncomfortable, nothing like the relationship they'd shared in the time she'd been here.

He'd brought her a palm tree and a fruity drink. His eyes had spoken of a love that invited her into something she'd never believed she could have.

She was doing what was best for both of them.

She had to tell him goodbye.

GABRIEL PARKED IN front of the motel room door and dreaded the goodbye that was to come. The sun was bright and the snow that had fallen the day before had been negligible. It was a beautiful day for a helicopter ride.

He'd brought Jordon to the motel room the night before and their ride from the hospital had been quiet, their only conversation dealing with the aftermath of the cases.

He now opened his car door and started to get out, but Jordon flew out of the door with her two bags in hand. "Don't get out," she said. "I've got this."

She opened the back door and threw her bags into the seat and then got into the car. She cast him a cheerful smile that only managed to break his heart just a little bit more.

"Thanks for taking me to the airport," she said.

"No problem," he replied and pulled out of the motel parking lot. "How are you feeling today?"

"Not too bad. I'm going to be sore for a while, but it's nothing I can't handle."

Her scent filled the car, evoking desire and love even as he drove her to the place where she'd leave him forever. Throughout the long night a weary resignation had set in. He loved…and he'd lost.

He couldn't make her love him if she didn't. He couldn't force her to understand that they belonged together if she didn't believe that in her very soul.

He could only let her go to find her own

kind of happiness. She was the bravest woman he knew and yet he still believed it was fear that held her back.

"Nice day to fly," he said. "And now you can take that vacation you've been waiting for. You've definitely earned it."

"What about you? When was the last time you had a vacation?" she asked.

"I haven't taken one since I took this job," he admitted. He wasn't going to tell her that the idea of going off somewhere alone simply wasn't appealing to him.

"I'd definitely say you've earned one, too."

Why were they talking about vacations when his heart ached so badly? He didn't want inane conversation and yet he knew that was all that was left between them.

They reached the small airport, and as he parked, he had a perfect view of the helicopter that waited to take her home. "Looks like your ride is here."

"You don't have to get out." She unbuckled her seat belt.

"I'll walk you to the door," he replied. Just like he had every night since she'd been attacked by Hannah and had gotten lost in the snowstorm.

He got out of the car and grabbed the larger bag from her. Silently they entered the airport and then exited to the tarmac, where the helicopter pilot stood waiting.

When he saw them approaching, he climbed into the plane and the blades began their whooping swirl as they prepared for takeoff. Jordon took her bag, and when she looked back up at Gabriel, her green eyes simmered with emotion.

"Gabriel, I can't thank you enough for everything you've done for me while I've been here," she said.

"Jordon, I…"

She held up a hand. "Please don't say anything. This is hard enough already. Goodbye, Gabriel."

She didn't wait for his reply. She hurried to the helicopter door and climbed inside. He backed away, grief ripping another hole in his heart.

The helicopter blades spun faster and the engine began to whine. An empty, hollow wind blew through him as he turned to go back to the parking lot. It had taken him so long to finally find the woman he wanted forever in his life and now she was gone.

"Gabriel!"

His name carried on the breeze and he turned around to see her running toward him. Had she forgotten something? When she reached him, she threw her arms around his neck and smiled up at him.

"I want it," she said. Her eyes sparkled with a light that half stole his breath away. "I want life with you. I thought I could just walk away from you, but I can't. I love you, Gabriel, and I'm willing to take a chance on us."

He couldn't speak. Instead he took her lips with his in a kiss that held all his hope, all his dreams and every ounce of his love for her.

"I'd wrap you up in my arms right now if you didn't have stitches in your back," he said when the kiss ended.

She laughed, that husky sound that delighted him. "I don't know how this is going to work, but I do know my vacation is going to be right here with you."

"What about the beach?"

"To heck with the beach. I want to spend my time wherever you are."

"I want that, Jordon," he replied fervently. "We're going to make this work. We'll figure it all out as long as we love each other."

"You know I'm messy and I don't cook."

"And I love that about you," he assured her.

She cast a quick glance back at the helicopter. "I've got to go."

"I know." He kissed her again and this time

he tasted her love for him and the promise of a future together. "I'll call you."

"I'll be waiting." She backed away from him and then turned and ran back and disappeared into the helicopter.

Gabriel remained in place and watched as the bird lifted off to carry her away. He missed her already, but his heart was filled with a wealth of happiness.

The sun glinted on the helicopter as it circled the airport once, and the shine was warm in Gabriel's heart. He loved and she loved him back, and he'd never been more certain of his future.

She might not know it yet, but Jordon was the woman he was going to marry. She was the woman who would have his children.

This wasn't a goodbye; it was only the beginning. He had no doubt in his mind that life with Jordon would be a wonderful adventure and he was more than up for the challenge.

Epilogue

The sun was hot in Florida in late August. Jordon sat on the chaise lounge and sighed with happiness. "This is positively wonderful," she said as she closed her eyes and raised her face.

"You just think it's wonderful because you have a handsome devil to rub sunscreen on your back," Gabriel said as his hands sensually worked the coconut-scented cream across her skin.

"You're right—the beach is definitely better with you," she replied.

He kissed the back of her neck and shivers of pleasure worked up her spine. "If you keep doing that we won't have much time in the sun. We'll wind up back in the room like we have done every afternoon since we arrived here."

He laughed and moved back to his chair

next to hers. "Vacations are definitely better with a snuggle buddy."

She looked at him and grinned. "You're a great snuggle buddy." She leaned back in her chair and closed her eyes once again.

There were still moments when she needed to pinch herself to make sure this was real and not a dream. The last six months had been magical.

She and Gabriel had taken every opportunity to see each other despite the distance. She'd spent weekends at his house and he'd come to Kansas City every chance he got and had stayed with her.

Each and every day their love had only grown deeper, her confidence in what they had together grew stronger. He had made her believe in herself in a way nobody had ever done before. He made her a better woman and she liked to believe she made him a better man.

She hadn't been surprised when he'd told her Joan and Ted Overton had decided to remain in Branson and continue to run Diamond Cove. The couple had decided that despite their heartbreak over Hannah's crimes, they couldn't allow her plot to succeed.

She'd been happy when Gabriel had told her that the couple appeared to be closer than ever, and while they planned to support their daughter, they also believed she belonged behind bars.

"Whew, it's really hot out here," Gabriel said, pulling her from her thoughts with a seductive lilt to his voice. "I'll bet our room is nice and cool. We could probably crank up a little music and dance in our underwear in the air-conditioning."

Jordon laughed, but didn't open her eyes. "You definitely look hot dancing in your underwear," she replied. She was so in love with this man.

"If we go inside we could probably even request room service to bring us a bottle of champagne to celebrate."

She turned her head to look at him. "And what would we be celebrating?"

He swung his legs over the side of his chair to face her and pulled their beach tote bag closer to him. His ocean-blue eyes gazed at her softly. "Jordon, these last six months have been the happiest I've ever been in my life."

Her heart squeezed. "You know I feel the same way. I thought I knew what love was, but it took you to really show me what it's all about."

"You know I'm all in with you, Jordon."

"Since you put in your resignation and are

going to be part of the men in blue in Kansas City and move in with me next month, you'd better be all in," she said with a laugh.

"The real question is, are you sure you're really all in?" He slipped a hand into the tote bag and pulled out a small velvet box.

Her breath caught in her throat and she sat up to face him as he got down on one knee in the sand. His eyes suddenly held a touch of uncertainty. He opened the ring box to display a sparkling princess-cut diamond ring. "Will you make me the happiest man in the world and marry me, Jordon?"

Her heart trembled inside her, not with fear, but rather with a kind of wild joy she'd never known before. "You silly man, take that worried look out of your eyes. Yes, yes, a thousand times yes, I'll marry you."

He slipped the ring on her finger and then pulled her up off the chaise and into his arms. The kiss they shared was filled with unbridled passion and enduring love.

"Hey, get a room," a male voice called from nearby.

She broke the kiss and turned her head to see a skinny old man eyeing them. She grinned at him. "We have a room and we're going there right now." She placed a hand over Gabriel's heart. "This is the man I'm going to have babies with."

The old man's lips turned up in a smile. "Then get off the beach before you start that kind of business."

"Come on, fiancé. You heard what he said," she said to Gabriel.

He grasped her hand and together they ran across the sand toward the hotel, toward their future filled with love and laughter and family.

* * * * *

LARGER-PRINT BOOKS!

HARLEQUIN

Presents®

PASSION GUARANTEED SEDUCTION

GET 2 FREE LARGER-PRINT
NOVELS PLUS 2 FREE GIFTS!

YES! Please send me 2 FREE LARGER-PRINT Harlequin Presents® novels and my 2 FREE gifts (gifts are worth about $10). After receiving them, if I don't wish to receive any more books, I can return the shipping statement marked "cancel." If I don't cancel, I will receive 6 brand-new novels every month and be billed just $5.30 per book in the U.S. or $5.74 per book in Canada. That's a saving of at least 12% off the cover price! It's quite a bargain! Shipping and handling is just 50¢ per book in the U.S. and 75¢ per book in Canada.* I understand that accepting the 2 free books and gifts places me under no obligation to buy anything. I can always return a shipment and cancel at any time. Even if I never buy another book, the two free books and gifts are mine to keep forever.

176/376 HDN GHVY

Name _____ (PLEASE PRINT)

Address _____ Apt. #

City _____ State/Prov. _____ Zip/Postal Code

Signature (if under 18, a parent or guardian must sign)

Mail to the **Reader Service:**
IN U.S.A.: P.O. Box 1867, Buffalo, NY 14240-1867
IN CANADA: P.O. Box 609, Fort Erie, Ontario L2A 5X3

**Are you a subscriber to Harlequin Presents® books
and want to receive the larger-print edition?
Call 1-800-873-8635 today or visit us at www.ReaderService.com.**

* Terms and prices subject to change without notice. Prices do not include applicable taxes. Sales tax applicable in N.Y. Canadian residents will be charged applicable taxes. Offer not valid in Quebec. This offer is limited to one order per household. Not valid for current subscribers to Harlequin Presents Larger-Print books. All orders subject to credit approval. Credit or debit balances in a customer's account(s) may be offset by any other outstanding balance owed by or to the customer. Please allow 4 to 6 weeks for delivery. Offer available while quantities last.

Your Privacy—The Reader Service is committed to protecting your privacy. Our Privacy Policy is available online at www.ReaderService.com or upon request from the Reader Service.

We make a portion of our mailing list available to reputable third parties that offer products we believe may interest you. If you prefer that we not exchange your name with third parties, or if you wish to clarify or modify your communication preferences, please visit us at www.ReaderService.com/consumerchoice or write to us at Reader Service Preference Service, P.O. Box 9062, Buffalo, NY 14240-9062. Include your complete name and address.

LARGER-PRINT BOOKS!
GET 2 FREE LARGER-PRINT NOVELS PLUS
2 FREE GIFTS!

HARLEQUIN®

Romance

From the Heart, For the Heart

YES! Please send me 2 FREE LARGER-PRINT Harlequin® Romance novels and my 2 FREE gifts (gifts are worth about $10). After receiving them, if I don't wish to receive any more books, I can return the shipping statement marked "cancel." If I don't cancel, I will receive 4 brand-new novels every month and be billed just $5.09 per book in the U.S. or $5.49 per book in Canada. That's a savings of at least 15% off the cover price! It's quite a bargain! Shipping and handling is just 50¢ per book in the U.S. and 75¢ per book in Canada.* I understand that accepting the 2 free books and gifts places me under no obligation to buy anything. I can always return a shipment and cancel at any time. Even if I never buy another book, the two free books and gifts are mine to keep forever.

119/319 HDN GHWC

Name _____ (PLEASE PRINT)

Address _____ Apt. #

City _____ State/Prov. _____ Zip/Postal Code

Signature (if under 18, a parent or guardian must sign)

Mail to the **Reader Service:**
IN U.S.A.: P.O. Box 1867, Buffalo, NY 14240-1867
IN CANADA: P.O. Box 609, Fort Erie, Ontario L2A 5X3

Want to try two free books from another line?
Call 1-800-873-8635 or visit www.ReaderService.com.

* Terms and prices subject to change without notice. Prices do not include applicable taxes. Sales tax applicable in N.Y. Canadian residents will be charged applicable taxes. Offer not valid in Quebec. This offer is limited to one order per household. Not valid for current subscribers to Harlequin Romance Larger-Print books. All orders subject to credit approval. Credit or debit balances in a customer's account(s) may be offset by any other outstanding balance owed by or to the customer. Please allow 4 to 6 weeks for delivery. Offer available while quantities last.

Your Privacy—The Reader Service is committed to protecting your privacy. Our Privacy Policy is available online at www.ReaderService.com or upon request from the Reader Service.

We make a portion of our mailing list available to reputable third parties that offer products we believe may interest you. If you prefer that we not exchange your name with third parties, or if you wish to clarify or modify your communication preferences, please visit us at www.ReaderService.com/consumerschoice or write to us at Reader Service Preference Service, P.O. Box 9062, Buffalo, NY 14240-9062. Include your complete name and address.

HRLP15

WESTERN WP PROMISES

YES! Please send me **The Western Promises Collection** in Larger Print. This collection begins with 3 FREE books and 2 FREE gifts (gifts valued at approx. $14.00 retail) in the first shipment, along with the other first 4 books from the collection! If I do not cancel, I will receive 8 monthly shipments until I have the entire 51-book Western Promises collection. I will receive 2 or 3 FREE books in each shipment and I will pay just $4.99 US/ $5.89 CDN for each of the other four books in each shipment, plus $2.99 for shipping and handling per shipment. *If I decide to keep the entire collection, I'll have paid for only 32 books, because 19 books are FREE! I understand that accepting the 3 free books and gifts places me under no obligation to buy anything. I can always return a shipment and cancel at any time. My free books and gifts are mine to keep no matter what I decide.

272 HCN 3070 472 HCN 3070

Name	(PLEASE PRINT)	
Address		Apt. #
City	State/Prov.	Zip/Postal Code
Signature (if under 18, a parent or guardian must sign)		

Mail to the **Reader Service:**

IN U.S.A.: P.O. Box 1867, Buffalo, NY 14240-1867
IN CANADA: P.O. Box 609, Fort Erie, Ontario L2A 5X3

* Terms and prices subject to change without notice. Prices do not include applicable taxes. Sales tax applicable in N.Y. Canadian residents will be charged applicable taxes. This offer is limited to one order per household. All orders subject to approval. Credit or debit balances in a customer's account(s) may be offset by any other outstanding balance owed by or to the customer. Please allow 4 to 6 weeks for delivery. Offer available while quantities last. Offer not available to Quebec residents.

Your Privacy—The Reader Service is committed to protecting your privacy. Our Privacy Policy is available online at www.ReaderService.com or upon request from the Reader Service.

We make a portion of our mailing list available to reputable third parties that offer products we believe may interest you. If you prefer that we not exchange your name with third parties, or if you wish to clarify or modify your communication preferences, please visit us at www.ReaderService.com/consumerchoice or write to us at Reader Service Preference Service, P.O. Box 9062, Buffalo, NY 14240-9062. Include your complete name and address.

WPBPA16R

LARGER-PRINT BOOKS!
GET 2 FREE LARGER-PRINT NOVELS PLUS
2 FREE GIFTS!

HARLEQUIN®

super romance®

More Story...More Romance